FRAGMENTED SKIES

The Last Chronicles of Earth

Waylen D Govall

S.D.N Publishing

CONTENTS

THE ANALYST

CHAPTER 1: THE ANOMALY

Dr. Sarah Geller sat before a cluster of screens in the labyrinthine expanse of the high-tech observatory, her eyes darting between lines of data and intricate graphs. Each numerical entry was a discrete universe, concealing immeasurable consequences within its sterile form. And as she surveyed this digital ocean, a peculiar wave arose—a deviation in the data. A discrepancy so slight, it might have been dismissed as an aberration in another context. But not here. Not with a comet racing through the solar system at an alarmingly unpredictable trajectory.

Sarah Geller had always been an epistemological fortress, valuing data over dogma. With a doctoral degree in Astrophysics and a research portfolio that had been cited in countless scientific journals, she had climbed her way to the position of senior data analyst at this facility. Her role was indispensable but largely confined to shadows, as her work rarely left the classified echo chambers of space research. She was the last sieve through which any data would pass before influencing international policies or provoking collective human action.

The anomaly she detected lay in the astrophysical models she had grown to trust. These models, built on decades of astronomical observations and computational refinement, had started to diverge from the real-time data collected by the facility's telescopes. Initial disbelief urged her to review the instrumentation. She conducted diagnostic tests, initiated recalibrations, and consulted with software engineers to rule out any technological flaws. Yet the deviation remained, immutable and irrefutable.

The moment had come to escalate the matter. Sarah switched her screen to an internal communication portal and punched in the codes that would direct her message to her core team: Dr. Fred Amana, systems analyst, and Dr. Lisa Ming, computational astrophysicist. Within minutes, both were in her office, peering over her shoulders at the unsettling discrepancy on her monitors. Skepticism contoured their faces until they each took turns verifying the data themselves. Their initial incredulity waned, replaced by a dawning realization that their unassuming colleague had stumbled upon something monumentally troubling.

Inside her, a cauldron of emotions simmered. An ambivalence entangled in cobwebs of scientific integrity and human apprehension. On the one hand, she was professionally conditioned to seek anomalies, to thrust the paradigms of human understanding into broad daylight. On the other, she recognized the disquieting implications of her discovery. For if her calculations were accurate—and every nerve in her body told her they were—this data was an unequivocal confirmation of the comet's cataclysmic course towards Earth.

The situation called for one final due diligence. She couldn't afford to perpetuate an apocalyptic theory based on a set of observations, no matter how compelling. The hypothesis had to be ironclad, and for that, Sarah had developed a proprietary algorithm—a complex weave of statistical methods and error analyses designed to cross-verify observational data against theoretical models. It was the closest thing to an irrefutable stamp of scientific credibility, and it was a tool she reserved for the most critical of assessments.

She initiated the algorithm, watching as her screens flickered with new arrays of numbers, each calculation a minute ripple in a sea of variables. The tension in the room was as palpable as it was unspoken. All eyes were on the monitors, on the swirling helixes of data crunching and recrunching itself, searching for a pattern that could either confirm or dispel their deepest fears. And as Sarah initiated the last sequence, a part of her hoped, almost desperately, for a miraculous divergence—a last-minute reprieve that would dismantle the looming omen. But another part of her, the scientist, yearned for consistency, for the anomaly to survive the algorithm's gauntlet, and to emerge as a newly minted fact.

As the processing bar inched towards completion, Sarah understood that her next actions could seal the fate not just of her career but of an entire planet's future. A double-click would execute the final run of the algorithm, and an enter key would transmit the result to the world. It was a strangely surreal moment, poised between possibilities. Sarah felt as if she were both particle and wave, localized in her purpose but extended in her potential impact, a Schrödinger's cat of cosmic import.

Her finger descended on the mouse, double-clicking with a finality that belied her internal turmoil. The computational cogs turned for what felt like an eternity, then halted. On her screen, a series of numbers appeared, unambiguous and irrevocable. She glanced at them, her breath catching in her throat. The anomaly had survived the algorithm. It was real. It was coming.

The room remained silent. All sounds seemed to have been swallowed by the gravity of the moment, by the profound, almost mystical enormity of what they had all participated in uncovering. And as Sarah Geller looked at the screen again, her eyes lingering on the newly birthed data point, she knew —this was not merely a scientific discovery but a primal acknowledgment of their entanglement in the intricate web of cosmic events. Earth-shattering in both the metaphorical and the literal sense, the data before her bore the somber weight of inevitable truth.

CHAPTER 2:
IRREFUTABLE PROOF

The room remained as silent as the vacuum of space, each person individually processing the numerical reality staring back at them. It was a rare moment when data transcended its quantifiable boundaries to become something almost sentient —like a spectral whisper that only Dr. Sarah Geller and her colleagues could hear. A chill cut through the sterile atmosphere, one borne not from the air conditioning but from the foreboding realization of what they had just confirmed.

It was Sarah who broke the silence. "I'll prepare the report. This needs to escalate immediately." Her voice was as unwavering as the data on the screen—unchangeable and dictating a fixed future path. She encrypted the files and uploaded them to the observatory's secure server, from where they would be accessible only to a handful of individuals worldwide who had the clearance and the intellectual acumen to comprehend their significance.

While the file was uploading, her computer blinked with a new incoming message. It was from her immediate superior, Dr. Jack Orville, the head of Astrophysical Research at the facility. The message was laconic: "Dr. Geller, join me for an urgent meeting. Room 301. J.O." Room 301 was equipped with secure communication systems, usually reserved for classified discussions of the highest order. Sarah knew that her discovery had just graduated from a departmental enigma to an institutional crisis.

The meeting was tense but conspicuously devoid of panic—an island of stoicism amid a rising tide of inevitable chaos. Sarah outlined her findings, taking the team through the intricate technicalities of her algorithms, her cross-checks, and the final, irrefutable data point that affirmed the comet's collision course with Earth. The room listened in focused silence, the gravitas of the situation enunciating each technical term and mathematical model into a sort of solemn scientific liturgy. When she finished, Dr. Orville looked up from his tablet and spoke, "Your work will form the basis for Project Helios." No further details were given, adding another layer of opacity to the labyrinth of classified information.

Sarah returned to her workspace, where Fred and Lisa awaited her. Before she could say anything, her phone buzzed. It was a news alert. "BREAKING: Rumors of Imminent Cosmic Collision Spark Global Concern." Despite the observatory's best efforts to contain the information, it had leaked. Somewhere in the circuit of closed-loop discussions, firewalls, and confidential memos, a crack had appeared. And through that crack, the whispers of apocalypse had begun to infect public consciousness.

Almost immediately, Dr. Orville sent another message, summoning her once again to Room 301. This time the atmosphere was tinged with suspicion. Sarah was interrogated about the leak, an exercise she found both redundant and insulting. She had devoted her life to this work, to the ethical conduct of science, and the implication that she could be responsible for such a breach was not just offensive—it was ludicrous. Her data integrity was her professional identity. "I've only discussed my findings with those who needed to know," she assured them.

"We believe you, Dr. Geller," Dr. Orville finally conceded. "Your findings will still form the cornerstone of Project Helios. However, you are now barred from any media interaction. Any and all communications about your data must be vetted through the public affairs department."

Sarah returned to her office, her mind a carousel of conflicting emotions. There was a strange dichotomy at play: a sense of professional accomplishment in having her data form the basis of something as crucial as Project Helios, juxtaposed against a vague betrayal that her information—once the epitome of scientific purity—was now shrouded in bureaucratic murkiness and public paranoia.

As she sat there, her monitors showing the real-time trajectory of the celestial body that had upended her life, Sarah thought about her role in this grand cosmic play. Her data, her irrefutable proof, had set into motion a chain of events far beyond her control, events whose endpoints she could neither predict nor influence. This mingling of exactitude and uncertainty, of scientific precision and existential ambiguity, encapsulated the paradox that was Dr. Sarah Geller. An analyst caught in the crossfire between her devotion to data and the unfathomable consequences that data could now unleash upon the world. And as she pondered this, one thing became clear: Her data was no longer just numbers on a screen; it was the prologue to an unwritten, and perhaps unwritable, chronicle of humankind's confrontation with the universe.

CHAPTER 3: SILENT PRELUDE TO CHAOS

Dr. Sarah Geller was back in her workspace, but this time her monitors displayed a surreal juxtaposition: complex scientific graphs on one screen and news feeds on the other. As she sat there, news channels buzzed with growing hysteria—analysts, theologians, and even psychics were dissecting the rumored end of days. Even without confirmation, the world was knitting its own tapestry of fear. The weird amalgamation of vindication and dread churned within her; her data had escaped the obsidian walls of theoretical models and was now an entity in the public consciousness.

Her colleagues had varied reactions. Dr. Fred Amana, normally so stoic, appeared frazzled. He gazed at the news feed, then at Sarah. "I guess we set the cat among the pigeons." Dr. Lisa Ming, on the other hand, was in awe. "The course of future history is in these numbers," she whispered, more to herself than anyone else. The situation was extraordinary, binding them in a common fate even as it isolated them in their unique confrontations with it.

Just then, another message from Dr. Orville appeared on Sarah's screen. She opened it and found an encrypted file attached. After multiple layers of authentication, the document revealed its contents: a finalized confirmation from other observatories and top governmental agencies around the world. The comet was on an irrevocable collision course with Earth. She was also offered a seat in an undisclosed survival bunker—a secret ark for select individuals to wait out the cataclysm. Her immediate response was to decline. It felt abhorrent to even consider such an option when so many others would not have that luxury. Plus, she had read the data on the size and mass of the approaching object. Trying to ride it out in a bunker was the equivalent of sitting at ground zero of a nuclear explosion protected by a cheap tent. Nevertheless she mulled the thought.

As the hours waned, Sarah came to a final decision. She would spend her remaining days at her post, collating as much data as possible about the celestial assassin. For what purpose, she could not say. It was as if she hoped that her information might serve some post-collision civilization or maybe even form the scientific foundation of a new world. Though she couldn't put her finger on why, it seemed crucial that someone document this cosmic tragedy in the language she knew best—numbers.

Evening settled over the observatory. Most of her colleagues had left, their faces pallid masks of worry as they departed to be with families or to seek solace in whatever way they could. Sarah chose to remain, gazing through the telescope at the comet—a mere smudge against the backdrop of stars, yet a harbinger of untold destruction.

As she was about to pack up, the door creaked open. In walked Manuel, a custodial worker whose face was as familiar as it was unremarkable. He had probably cleaned her office countless times without either of them acknowledging the other's presence. Tonight, however, their eyes met. "Mind if I take a look?" he asked, his voice tinged with an indescribable emotion. Sarah stepped aside, gesturing towards the telescope.

Manuel peered into the eyepiece for a minute that seemed to

stretch on forever, then finally looked up. He didn't say a word; none were needed. Sarah understood that Manuel, who perhaps couldn't tell a comet from a meteoroid, comprehended the gravity of the smudge he had just seen. It was an unspoken but profoundly human moment.

As both stood there, each lost in their thoughts, their titles meant nothing. Sarah Geller, Ph.D. in Astrophysics, and Manuel, the custodial worker, were just two individuals under the sky that was soon to be set ablaze. In that instant, they were bound not by data, not by the looming apocalypse, but by their shared and deeply human confrontation with the unfathomable.

Manuel reached into his pocket and pulled out a light green packet, offering the open end to Sarah. Sarah hesitated, about to shake her head, then changed her mind and accepted the proffered spearmint gum with a nod of appreciation.

Both stood in the observatory's dim light, their eyes turned upwards but their minds spiraling inwards, caught in a contemplative fugue. Words would have been inadequate, and so they shared the silence—a fitting elegy to the inexplicable cosmic tragedy that awaited them. If humanity's legacy was to be a whisper in the vast corridors of the universe, then perhaps there was no better prelude than this silent communion of souls, a quiet acknowledgment of the cosmic theater that had staged their existence and was now preparing to bring down the curtain.

THE LAST CANVAS

CHAPTER 4:
BRUSHSTROKES OF
DESPERATION

Yvonne stood in front of a virginal canvas, awash in the kaleidoscope of hues from her cluttered studio's palette. The room had a strange tranquility, unaffected by the frenzy gripping the world outside. Televisions blared, radio signals scrambled, and news sites bristled with speculative numbers—times, distances, survival rates. But in her studio, time seemed to elongate, as if the impending comet itself had given her a different, desperate kind of peace.

Her brush, poised just millimeters away from the canvas, trembled. How does one paint a valediction to the world? Each stroke seemed pretentious in its permanence. Art was meant to outlast its creator, but what when there was no 'outlasting'? Her brush retreated from the canvas, as if the weight of the blank space had suddenly grown too heavy to bear.

In a reckless moment, Yvonne dipped her brush into an amalgam of burnt sienna and titanium white and slashed it across the canvas. Her heart recoiled as the colors splayed into random geometries. It wasn't right; it was a scar, not a beginning. With a frustrated sigh, she tore the canvas off its easel and tossed it into a corner already cluttered with the casualties of similar attempts.

New canvas. New possibilities. But new also meant final. Her eyes drifted to the calendar. Every crossed-out day was a reminder that time was hurtling forward, as relentlessly as the celestial object threatening to extinguish all life.

As she pondered the next attempt, the door to her studio creaked open. Julia, a former student of hers and now a promising young artist, walked in. "I thought I'd find you here," she said, taking in the discarded canvases. "Working on a final masterpiece?"

Julia's words, meant to be light, fell heavily in the room's thick air. "A masterpiece assumes an audience," Yvonne responded, her voice brittle. "I'm not sure of either."

"But isn't that what art is about?" Julia ventured cautiously. "It's not about the applause or the critiques. It's about capturing a thought, an emotion, a moment, and making it eternal, even if that eternity is cut short."

Julia's words echoed through the room long after she left, reverberating through the spaces cluttered with brushes, tubes of paint, and unfinished canvases. Yvonne felt as if a fog had lifted. With newfound determination, she returned to her easel. Her hands no longer trembled. The question was no longer about what the world needed or wanted to see. This was about her voice, her vision, and her submission to the cataclysmic dance between creation and destruction.

Picking up a palette knife, she squeezed out azure, cobalt, and cerulean hues of paint, interspersed with dabs of white. Then she mixed them vigorously, the colors swirling into each other like some celestial dance. Armed with a new conviction, she approached the canvas.

This time, her brush met the canvas with courage. Bold strokes of cerulean blue flew across it, like a sky in turmoil or a restless sea. Each layer seemed to capture the paradox that was the world outside—beautiful yet destructive, soothing yet tempestuous. She didn't pause to judge or analyze; she let the form take shape, led more by her subconscious than by any deliberate thought.

Hours slid by unnoticed, her brush narrating a tale of its own. Finally, exhausted but content, she stepped back. Across the canvas lay an abstract vista—imprecise yet evocative, chaotic yet strangely tranquil. It was neither Earth nor comet, but an otherworldly landscape that seemed to encapsulate both. And across this landscape, a layer of frenzied cerulean blue danced—capturing the sublime beauty and terrifying power that was the cosmic visitor and the planet it threatened.

Yvonne washed her brushes, but the blue stains on her hands remained, as if permanently tattooed by this intimate engagement with her final canvas. She felt drained but strangely complete, as if this one piece had, in a surreal way, justified her existence, her life, and her art.

The painting wasn't complete, but it had a voice, a purpose, and a soul. It was her ultimate tribute to a world facing its curtain call —a visual elegy to both its splendor and its fragility. And as she looked at the bursts of cerulean, she knew that her final canvas had found its beginning.

CHAPTER 5: PALETTE OF MEMORIES

Resuming her work the next day, Yvonne felt an array of emotions flood her being. The canvas stared back at her, the abstract expanse of blues both inviting and challenging. She realized that her next strokes would be guided not just by the immediacy of the looming disaster but also by the entire spectrum of her life's experiences.

Picking up a brush laden with crimson, she hesitated before letting it touch the canvas. Memories began to surface, unbidden but insistent—flashes of her first art show, the exhilarating thrill of her first sale, the crushing weight of her first failure. The color began to flow from her brush, the vivid reds dispersing into the existing tapestry of blues, creating a pulsating, almost living, contrast. This was the hue of love lost, of relationships that once promised permanence but ended in ephemeral heartbreak.

She then mixed a shade of muted gray, the color of clouds on a rainy day, tinged with the patina of age. As the brush moved, it carried with it the echoes of opportunities missed, chances not taken, paths not chosen. The gray seeped into the canvas like an old photograph, its monochrome tones whispering of what could have been but never was.

Yet, as she navigated through her memories, she also stumbled upon moments of untarnated joy—tiny islands in the archipelago of her life that shone with a light of their own. With a lighter touch, she added radiant yellows, each stroke a testament to small victories, simple pleasures, and the bliss of the ordinary.

She stepped back, momentarily overwhelmed. Her canvas had become an intricate map, each color a coordinate in the geography of her existence. It was a visual memoir, abstracted to its emotional essence. A complex tapestry woven from the threads of a life fully lived, and now, perhaps, fully understood.

By now, the comet had become an undeniable smear of light in the daytime sky, its tail a shining trail that spoke both of its celestial beauty and its potential for destruction. Inspired, Yvonne delicately added a luminous streak of silver, cutting across her canvas like a scythe. It was a scar, a dissonant element, yet its brilliance only enhanced the emotional complexity of her painting. In its glaring luminescence, she saw the transience of all things—the fleeting nature of joy, love, sorrow, and ultimately, life itself.

Her canvas was a mélange of colors, each hue adding depth and dimension to the others. It was the most honest work she had ever done, the rawest, and perhaps because of that, the most beautiful. Here, in this final work, she had achieved something elusive, something she had been striving for throughout her artistic career—an honest reckoning with the human experience, not as she imagined it to be, but as she had lived it.

Stepping back, she reviewed her painting with a mixture of pride and melancholy. Her last work, her last will and testament to a world that was both glorious and flawed.

CHAPTER 6: THE EPHEMERAL GALLERY

The canvas in front of Yvonne had reached a point of almost being complete, yet still seemed to be whispering for a final touch. It was like a poem that begged for a conclusive stanza, a narrative pleading for its denouement. Though she had poured her past and present into it, it felt like the painting still awaited its future—its final communion with the world.

Just then, the television in the corner of her studio sprung to life, automatically triggered by a government alert. The grim-faced announcer confirmed what everyone had feared but secretly hoped would never materialize: the comet was now mere hours away from Earth. The collision was inevitable; human history would conclude in an astronomical full stop.

Yvonne felt her heart leap into her throat. She thought of her friends, her family, the strangers she'd never meet, and the places she'd never visit. A wave of temptation washed over her to abandon her project, to rush outside and experience the world one last time, to look up at the sky and wait. It felt selfish now to be locked away in a studio when the narrative of humanity was nearing its epilogue.

But as her eyes shifted back to her painting, it struck her. The canvas was her world now. It was her voice, her legacy, her final contribution to a cosmos that was far bigger and older than the comet, or Earth, or even humanity itself. Her art was not an act of defiance, but rather an act of existence, a declaration that she had lived, felt, loved, and pondered the questions that have no answers.

With a newfound tranquility, a calm urgency, she picked up her brush one last time. Her hands moved deftly, instilling life into the voids that still clung to the canvas. A few strokes here—adding depth to the sky, another stroke there—instilling a nuance to the chaotic swirls. The tiny changes subtly transformed the painting, as if each brushstroke was a word, and she was editing the final sentence of a long novel.

Finally, she dipped her brush into jet-black ink and signed her name in the corner. The simple act felt monumentally different this time. It was both an end and a beginning; the final period in the last chapter of a book, yet also the invitation to a reader to start from the beginning again. She stood back and studied her work. For the first time, she felt that it was complete. It was the truest reflection of her soul, a mirror into her complex relationship with a world that was both breathtakingly beautiful and achingly cruel.

Feeling that her work was finally ready to face the world, she carefully lifted the canvas off its easel and dressed herself in a coat. Carrying her final masterpiece, she stepped outside her studio, locking the door behind her. Her footsteps led her to the town square—a place where she had witnessed countless festivals, protests, celebrations, and gatherings. Today, it was different. The atmosphere was thick with an ineffable blend of dread and hope, resignation and wonder. People were holding their loved ones, their eyes collectively gazing upwards at the nearing celestial body, its tail now a brilliant river of light in the sky.

With a quiet resolve, she placed her painting in the middle of the square and stepped back. Almost immediately, people began to gather around it. Some took out their phones to capture the artwork, perhaps the last piece of human creativity they would ever witness. Others simply stared, lost in its intricate mélange of colors, each finding their own meanings in its abstract depths.

As she stood there, Yvonne felt an overwhelming sense of fulfillment wash over her. Her art had started its ultimate journey. It was no longer hers; it now belonged to the world. For those few remaining hours, her canvas became an ephemeral gallery for humanity, a space where people could escape, however momentarily, from their collective fate, and find a sliver of beauty amidst imminent destruction. And in that brief intersection of time and space, she felt a connection with humanity that was as profound as it was short-lived, like a fleeting brushstroke in the grand, tragic, beautiful artwork that was life.

Yvonne turned her eyes towards the sky, joining the communal gaze of her species for the final act. She was ready.

JUNKYARD OF DREAMS

CHAPTER 7: RUSTY BEGINNINGS

Sam rifled through a pile of discarded electronics, his hands coated in grime and years of neglect that the junkyard had suffered. As an ex-engineer laid off in the automation wave, he possessed a discerning eye, honing in on tiny pieces of tech that could be repurposed for something useful. In a landscape full of rusting vehicles, mangled home appliances, and the detritus of a society that worshipped disposability, he was an alchemist turning base metal into gold.

The sky above was an uneasy gray, perhaps contemplating whether to unleash rain or simply maintain its overcast gloom. A drone buzzed high above, its mechanical eye capturing the grim terrain for reasons Sam could only speculate. But it wasn't the sky or the drone that troubled him; it was the impending celestial cataclysm, the world-ending comet that even the most sophisticated nations couldn't deflect.

Unfazed by doomsday prophecies and government advisories, Sam considered the sprawling junkyard his arena and lifeline. A cornucopia of forgotten technology, it was perfect for a man of his skills. Acres of vehicular corpses, mountains of shattered screens, and a sea of innumerable machine parts stretched out like a testament to humanity's wasteful extravagance. Now, in these end-times, they were the building blocks of survival. His survival.

Sam's thoughts were abruptly interrupted when a clang echoed from the other side of a pile of crushed cars. Cautiously, he placed the circuit board he was examining into his sack and moved stealthily to investigate. A group of five men, scruffy and armed with makeshift weapons, were scavenging—no, looting—a newly dumped heap of electronic waste. Their demeanor was far from Sam's careful and calculated approach. These men were opportunists, reveling in the lawlessness that the impending cataclysm had triggered.

Unlike Sam, who saw the junkyard as a place to build a future however brief, they treated it like a treasure trove to pillage, their actions fueled by a nihilistic acceptance of the apocalypse. They took what they wanted, not what they needed, recklessly dismantling items and discarding them, laughter punctuating their destructive spree. It angered Sam to see resources so frivolously wasted, especially when those very resources were finite and invaluable now more than ever.

In a world gasping for its last breaths, resources were power, and Sam knew he couldn't let this band of vandals take that away. A confrontation would be unwise; they outnumbered him and were armed. Instead, Sam sketched a mental note of what they were looting. He would have to revise his inventory list and perhaps redesign some of his shelter plans. It was a setback, but then, his entire life had been about overcoming setbacks, from losing his engineering job to surviving a divorce. What was an apocalypse if not just another bump in the road?

The rivals had grabbed solar panels and batteries, items Sam had earmarked for his energy system. With a grim sigh, he pulled out his notepad, crossing out items he knew he no longer had access to and adding others that could serve as alternative options.

As he recalibrated, he understood the urgency. Time was running out faster than calculations could predict. He had to act swiftly, efficiently, and maybe a little slyly if he were to complete his makeshift haven. The junkyard had always been a chaotic tapestry of humankind's material legacy. But in its rusting piles and decaying mounds, Sam saw potential; the raw elements needed for survival, and perhaps, just perhaps, for a rebirth.

His eyes fixed on the dimming horizon. Soon it would be night, and under the shroud of darkness, he would initiate the next phase. If this world was to end in fire and fury, Sam was intent on riding out the storm, cocooned in a fortress of forgotten things. With renewed resolve, he picked up a salvaged piece of rebar, using it to sketch new designs in the dirt floor. He would have to be quick, he would have to be smart, and above all, he would have to be resourceful. The clock was ticking, not just for him, but for humanity. And while he couldn't save the world, he was damn well going to save himself.

CHAPTER 8: BLUEPRINTS FOR SURVIVAL

Sam retreated to his makeshift "office," a repurposed shipping container he had outfitted with a table made from an old wooden door and a chair salvaged from a defunct office building. Across the walls were tacked blueprints, designs, and handwritten notes outlining what would be his crowning achievement: a self-sustaining shelter constructed entirely from the remnants of a discarded society.

Calculations filled the margins of his sketches, detailing the angles and materials required to best maintain insulation, how to angle the salvaged solar panels to catch the maximum amount of sunlight, and even a rudimentary rainwater collection system. Sam's fingers hovered above his dog-eared notebook as he calculated the weight distribution of his envisioned structure. In a world on the brink of calamity, this cramped space had become a sanctuary of logic and foresight.

It wasn't just about building a roof over his head. That would be too straightforward for a man of Sam's capabilities. His design incorporated an energy capture-and-storage system, water purification facilities, and even a compact hydroponic farm for food. It was meant to be a lifeboat, a sliver of habitability in a sea of impending desolation.

The table was littered with objects that were ordinary in appearance but extraordinary in utility. Strips of sheet metal salvaged from dismantled automobiles, rubber tires he planned to shred and use as insulation, solar panels torn from discarded garden lights, car batteries in various states of decay, and an array of screws, nuts, and bolts that would serve as the skeletal framework of his haven. Each piece of detritus was carefully cataloged and labeled, its purpose delineated in Sam's intricate plans.

However, a problem gnawed at him. His plans had hit a snag. The specific type of battery he needed for his sustainable energy system—a deep-cycle marine battery known for its durability and long life—was missing from his inventory. He had seen one just a week ago in a heap of automotive scraps, but when he went to retrieve it, the spot was empty. His quiet competitors, the band of opportunistic scavengers, had evidently recognized its value and claimed it first.

Frustration bubbled within him, but frustration was a luxury he couldn't afford. His mind pivoted towards solutions. His first option was to redesign the entire energy system, but that could take days he didn't have. Time was a currency in rapid depreciation. He estimated the comet's collision was days, if not hours away, and each tick of the clock whittled away his chances of completing the shelter in time.

The second option was riskier. He knew the general area where the rival group stored their haul. It was a gamble, laden with danger and the threat of violent confrontation. But it could also solve his problem swiftly, reinstating his original timeline.

Decision made, Sam reached for a different set of blueprints. These weren't plans for a shelter or a sustainable future, but for something far more immediate. They were blueprints for a makeshift EMP device, capable of frying electronic locks from a distance. If he could disable their security measures—even for a few minutes—he could retrieve the battery and vanish before they knew what happened.

He looked at the disassembled microwave on a shelf, its magnetron already eyed for its next life as part of the EMP generator. With precise movements, fueled by a lifetime of mechanical intuition, Sam began the process of transmuting one man's junk into another man's lifesaving technology. It was a risky move in a game with the highest stakes imaginable. Yet, as the blueprints took physical form on his worktable, Sam felt a surge of something that had become increasingly rare in this terminal world: hope.

Under the pall of a darkening sky, where the stars themselves seemed to dim in resignation, Sam began his meticulous preparations. In this cavern of repurposed objects and repurposed dreams, he was ready to do whatever it took to keep his aspirations from turning to dust. After all, in a world teetering on the edge of apocalypse, adaptability was not just a skill; it was the ultimate currency.

Thus, with a sense of weighted resolve, he picked up his newly constructed EMP device and tucked it into his bag next to an array of tools he might need. Tonight would be pivotal. Tonight, his blueprint for survival would be put to the ultimate test.

CHAPTER 9: FORGING TOMORROW

Time was an elastic concept, stretching taut as Sam prepared for his nocturnal operation. The junkyard was a labyrinth of towering metallic structures, eerily quiet save for the rustling of nocturnal creatures and the distant laughter of the rival scavengers. Armed with his makeshift EMP device, a bag of tools, and an unyielding resolve, Sam navigated through the darkened maze toward his objective.

He paused intermittently, taking cover behind heaps of scrap metal, ensuring he went undetected. A prickling sensation of both anticipation and dread skated along his nerves, but he channeled it into focus. His eyes settled on the enclosure where the rival scavengers stored their loot, illuminated only by the half-hearted glow of a salvaged streetlamp. Shadows danced like restless specters across the motley collection of car parts, electronics, and invaluable batteries—the one among them he specifically sought to retrieve.

Silently, Sam activated his EMP device, its core humming as it discharged, targeting the electronic lock that safeguarded the enclosure. With a pop and a flicker, the lock's interface dimmed out. His heart pounded; the plan had worked, at least this initial part. Swiftly, he maneuvered through the opening, his eyes scanning the collection until they landed on the deep-cycle marine battery—his prize. He hoisted it with grunting effort into his sack and retraced his steps, vanishing into the junkyard's maze just as the electronic lock flickered back to life.

Minutes later, he was back at his shipping container, breathing in shaky gulps, sweat matting his forehead. There was no time for relief or celebration. He set the retrieved battery on his table and got to work.

The construction process was an orchestra of clattering metal, whirring drills, and Sam's own occasional muttered curses. Days became a blur as he measured, cut, and joined pieces; installed the solar panels; secured the water purification system; and rigged up his hydroponic garden. Every decision, every action was dictated by an amalgam of engineering expertise and sheer improvisational skill. His hands were raw, his body ached, and sleep was a distant memory, but as the comet inched closer to Earth, inch by inch, so did his project toward completion.

Finally, as if manifesting through sheer will and endless cups of stale coffee, the sturdy shelter stood completed. From the outside, it might have looked like a jumble of metal plates, rubber, and glass. Yet inside, it was a marvel of ingenuity: LED lights hung from the ceiling, rigged to the solar-powered battery system; an improvised air filter hummed quietly, and the initial sprouts in his hydroponic system promised sustenance.

In a moment of stillness, Sam surveyed his creation, his lifeboat. It was more than a structure; it was a symbol, cobbled together from society's refuse but every inch an epitome of human ingenuity and resilience. If he were to face the world's end, he would do so in a fort, a modern-day air raid shelter of his own making, a testament to mankind's ability to adapt, to improvise, to overcome.

As Sam tightened the final bolt, sealing the roof and declaring the project complete, he noticed a soft buzz. Another drone was flying overhead, its camera focused on his shelter. Maybe it was another opportunistic scavenger, or perhaps a government survey. Whoever it was, he thought, they were capturing the epitome of defiance in the face of certain doom. Unbeknownst to him, footage of his one-man shelter, pieced together from the fragments of a decaying civilization, was uploaded to the global network.

Sam stepped back, his eyes lingering on his completed sanctuary. A comet could bring an apocalypse, but it couldn't extinguish the drive to persist, to build, to forge ahead against insurmountable odds. The clock was ticking, but for the first time in a long time, Sam felt like he'd snatched a small victory from the jaws of impending defeat. In his junkyard of dreams, among the rusting carcasses of a bygone era, Sam had constructed his tomorrow.

RESONANCE

CHAPTER 10:
COMPOSITION

The concert hall was a cathedral of silence. Rows of empty seats stared back at Isabelle; their plush upholstery devoid of an audience to comfort. Her violin rested on her shoulder, as if awaiting instructions, while her bow hovered tentatively over the strings. Isabelle had spent years on stages just like this one, vibrating the air with compositions from Bach to Shostakovich, enacting rituals of sound that transcended time and geography. But now, the impending doom cast a spectral gloom over the hall. The comet's arrival was a death knell for humanity, and Isabelle found herself pondering the relevance of her art form in a world bracing for apocalypse.

She had always thought of music as a universal language, a distillation of human emotion and intellect into wavelengths of sound. But the universe itself seemed intent on silencing her art, rendering the concert halls, opera houses, and jazz clubs obsolete. What purpose did a sonata serve when set against the astronomical cataclysm that loomed over Earth? Did the vibrational harmony of her violin strings hold any resonance when mirrored against the cosmic disharmony of a world-destroying comet? Was there a place for Beethoven's symphonies or Coltrane's improvisations in the cosmic score, or were they mere human annotations, destined to be erased?

Her ruminations were disrupted by the sharp ping of her

smartphone. A news alert flashed on the screen: a confirmation from multiple sources that all attempts to divert the comet had failed. Earth's expiration date was now irrefutably set. The gravity of that message settled into her, uniting with the weight she had been carrying. It was as if the universe had just punctuated its own dissonant composition with a fortissimo of finality.

Yet, in that moment, a counterpoint emerged within her thoughts. If her art form was indeed a language, could it not articulate the bittersweet symphony of human existence even in the face of impending annihilation? After all, music had the power to elevate the mundane, make sense of the chaotic, and lend beauty to the tragic. Perhaps it wasn't about combating the inevitability but confronting it—acknowledging the cosmic dissonance while striving for a momentary resonance.

Determined, Isabelle approached her sheet music, spreading blank pages across her stand. Her bow struck the strings, each note a query sent into the emptiness of the hall, each chord a hypothesis formed in the language she knew best. She began to compose, not just a sequence of notes but an orchestration of human experience. A musical tapestry that wove together the joy and sorrow, the love and loss, the awe and dread. This composition wouldn't be a requiem but an anthem—a culmination of every pitch and timbre that humanity had ever discovered, resonated, or felt.

She wrote furiously, as if racing against the comet itself. Harmonies converged and diverged on the paper before her, musical phrases crystallizing into motifs, motifs spiraling into complex movements. She aimed to make each note a pixel in a grand sonic picture, each crescendo a brushstroke in an auditory landscape. Isabelle named her composition "Resonance," a title that would encapsulate her audacious ambition: to create a piece that could reverberate within the human soul even as the heavens portended doom.

CHAPTER 11:
ENSEMBLE

Isabelle became absorbed in her task, scribbling musical notations on parchment, her eyes flickering between the strings of her violin and the lined paper as if transmitting encrypted messages. Notes and rhythms flowed out of her like a forgotten language suddenly recalled. It was a struggle to articulate this final musical statement, this distillation of collective human emotions into a sequence of sonic vibrations. But it wasn't enough for this to be a solo endeavor. True resonance, she believed, needed diversity; a chorus of instrumental voices that could lend volume and depth to her vision.

Reaching out to her contacts, Isabelle discovered that a few of her musician friends were still in the city. A cellist named Maria, a pianist named Aaron, and a percussionist named Dev. They congregated in the concert hall, each bringing with them not just their instruments but also a unique interpretive flair that Isabelle knew was crucial for "Resonance" to achieve its lofty aim. As they settled in their seats, tuning their instruments and sharing brief pleasantries, Isabelle felt an uncanny sense of normalcy, as if for a moment the comet-streaked sky outside had ceased to be a concern.

"As you all know," Isabelle began, "we have a chance to create something important here. Our art may not alter celestial paths, but it has the power to resonate within the human psyche.

'Resonance' is an endeavor to harmonize our chaotic emotional landscapes as we grapple with the end."

Maria, Aaron, and Dev nodded, their eyes filled with a mixture of trepidation and excitement. They rehearsed the piece, their individual contributions blending into a nuanced tapestry of sound that reverberated through the hall. It was an arresting experience, one that seemed to defy the very laws of acoustics. The notes held an emotional valence, each a nucleus around which circled electrons of sadness, joy, nostalgia, love—every conceivable human emotion.

As the rehearsal proceeded, Isabelle sensed that the room itself appeared to vibrate at a higher frequency, a synchrony with the composition that seemed almost metaphysical. She pondered, almost Sagan-esque in her contemplation, whether the very atoms that comprised the hall, the city, and even the looming comet, were in some strange way participants in this grand concert. Were they, in their minuscule existences, also capable of resonance?

After hours of rehearsal that felt like both an eternity and a fleeting moment, they stopped. A few minor adjustments were needed. Isabelle introduced a sequence she believed would encapsulate the crescendo of human history, from its primitive origins to its spacefaring aspirations, and back to its impending cataclysmic end—a loop of joy and sorrow, triumph and defeat.

As her colleagues dispersed for the night, Isabelle sat alone for a moment, reviewing the sheets of music scattered around her. So much had changed since those first scrawled musings. "Resonance" was no longer a solo endeavor contained within the neurons firing in her brain. It had evolved into a collaborative masterpiece, drawing on the talents and interpretative depth of her ensemble. For the first time since the impending doom had darkened humanity's collective consciousness, Isabelle felt a renewed sense of unity. And with it came a weighty responsibility, a mandate to share this unity through the global veins of technology to an audience starved for any form of coherence.

Isabelle collected the scattered sheets, her mind buzzing with the harmonic potential of the upcoming performance. It was set to be Earth's swan song, a harmonious farewell encoded in musical notation. It wouldn't divert the comet or change the fate that hung like the sword of Damocles over the world. But it had the potential to be Earth's epitaph, a melodious line in the cosmic score. A final act of human resonance.

CHAPTER 12: HARMONY

Isabelle stood on the stage, bow and violin in hand, staring into the void of empty seats before her. But she was not alone. The cellist Maria, pianist Aaron, and percussionist Dev had taken their positions, each a fundamental voice in the choir of instruments that was about to sing out to the world. Cameras, wired to livestream the performance globally, hummed with anticipation. Isabelle felt a surge of something indescribable, a complex emotion that straddled the line between hope and despair.

With a slight nod to her colleagues, Isabelle lifted her bow. A digital countdown blinked into view on the large screen above the stage. The world was watching, and as the numbers descended to zero, she initiated the first stroke, activating the strings in a ripple of sound that danced intricately with the cello's deep murmur, the piano's harmonic chords, and the percussion's rhythmic heartbeat. The composition had begun, and the opening strains of "Resonance" spiraled out into the digital ether.

As they played, Isabelle sensed something extraordinary. It wasn't just that the hall seemed to drink in each note as though parched for harmonic sustenance; it was as though the Earth itself had paused, for just a fraction of a moment, in its orbital dance. The sensation was illusory but palpable, as though the planet had become a giant ear, tuned to the frequencies they produced. It was a moment of surreal peace, a temporary truce brokered through melody.

Simultaneously, the livestream carried their performance far and wide, infiltrating homes, cafes, bunkers, and public spaces. Screens glowed in the dusk of Beijing, the midday sun of New York, the dawn of Sydney. People paused to listen, some with tears streaming down their faces, others in stoic acceptance, and still others in a joyous embrace of the present. "Resonance" did not eradicate the anguish or the uncertainty, but for those few minutes, it created a collective emotional space, a shared experience that transcended borders, languages, and ideologies.

In those moments, interspersed between the strains of music that Isabelle and her ensemble were creating, were scenes of people holding hands, of old animosities momentarily forgotten, of children staring in wonder not just at the sky but also at the screens that brought them this unexpected gift of art. Social media lit up, not with discussions, but with heart emoticons and applause icons, a silent digital standing ovation from humanity.

As Isabelle coaxed the last note from her violin, letting it linger in the air until it was a mere echo, a silence descended. It was not the silence of absence but of completion, an auditory canvas filled with the afterglow of music. She lowered her bow and met the eyes of Maria, Aaron, and Dev. There were no words, but their faces spoke volumes.

Isabelle took a bow, not just for the absent audience in the hall but for the people around the world who had borne witness to this final artistic act. It was a bow of gratitude, a thank-you to humanity for the gift of music, for the ability to convey the inexpressible through sound, for the creation of art that had the power to touch hearts and minds alike.

As the digital applause continued to roll in, Isabelle felt an inexplicable sense of fulfillment. She had grappled with the relevance of her art form in the shadow of annihilation, questioning the role of beauty in a world destined for destruction. But as she stood there, taking in the moment, she realized that "Resonance" had achieved something astonishing. It had not altered cosmic destinies or rewritten physical laws, but it had forged a moment of planetary empathy, a shared emotional beat in the heart of humankind.

This musical moment wouldn't linger; it was as transient as the comet that would soon extinguish it. But the power of transience lay in its ability to focus the human experience into a point of overwhelming now, a singularity of feeling and existence. Her music, a product of uniquely human creativity and sensibility, had carved out a space for collective humanity to dwell, even if just briefly, in a harmony of their own making.

As the comet drew nearer in the sky, ever so bright and dominant, Isabelle left the stage. Her composition, a finite series of notes in an infinitely complex universe, had been her final statement, a declaration that even in the face of cosmic indifference, humanity could produce a melody, a resonance, that was uniquely its own. And so, the comet came, not as a conqueror to a vanquished world, but as a cosmic player taking its turn in the great symphony of existence. The curtains closed.

MACHINATIONS

CHAPTER 13: THE COUNCIL OF DOOM

Senator Elaine Mathews' eyes scanned the room—a hidden bunker, austere in design yet rampant with screens that displayed unsettling, almost apocalyptic, data streams. The seriousness of the situation was not lost on her, nor on the military and political figures who shuffled about, murmuring in hushed voices.

The data on the screens, however, wasn't news to Elaine; she had just received a confidential file that divulged far more than these grim statistics. It was the sort of information that could induce mass hysteria—a detailed comet trajectory, odds of survival, and government countermeasures, all far more disheartening than the sanitized version the public had been given.

She sat down, her fingers absently caressing the screen of her encrypted tablet, where the file still lay open. For decades, she had been a linchpin in the intricate machine of politics. Her rise had not been devoid of morally gray decisions, Machiavellian tactics that still echoed in her conscience. Each compromise and calculated move had got her a seat at this table—a table that was now tantamount to a council of doom.

Elaine pondered over the labyrinthine dilemma she was entangled in. She could leak this information, shatter the opaque glass through which the government viewed its citizens, and possibly alert a public kept in ignorance. Such a path was fraught with risk, certainly one that could herald the end of her political career. It was a move that would infuriate her colleagues, who would see it as a betrayal not just to them but to a broader system of governance that thrived on information asymmetry.

Alternatively, she could stay silent, adhere to her long-standing allegiance to the power structures that had so faithfully served her. That choice, however, seemed increasingly untenable. She could feel it—an evolution in her principles, a divergence from the cold, calculated woman she had been to someone who sought a form of redemption in the final acts of a dying world.

While her mind was a theater of competing rationales, her fingers had already made the decision. They danced across the tablet's screen, navigating through firewalls and encryptions like a seasoned hacker. In a matter of seconds, she had uploaded the classified files to an encrypted server. Only one person knew of its existence and how to access it—a journalist with a track record of exposing governmental subterfuge, and a reputation for protecting their sources.

Elaine felt a shiver course through her spine as she pressed the final button, confirming the upload. The quiet of the bunker seemed to intensify, as if reacting to her decision. For a moment, she felt as if the walls were closing in on her, each inch a measurement of her shrinking political future. But then, almost as quickly, it dissipated, leaving behind a strange sort of tranquility. It was as if she had just navigated a minefield, aware that her next steps would be just as perilous, but for the first time, unburdened by the weight of deceit.

There was no turning back now. The wheels had been set in motion for a seismic shift in the public discourse about the impending cataclysm. Her decision, whether seen as heroic transparency or reckless endangerment, was irrevocable. Elaine Mathews, seasoned senator and masterful political operator, had just made the most dangerous move of her life—and the consequences, whatever they may be, were hurtling toward her like a comet in the night sky.

CHAPTER 14: UNEARTHED SECRETS

Within hours, the secret Elaine had released into the ether became the nucleus of a firestorm. Screens in the bunker flashed with breaking news—every channel, every website, bearing the same headline: "Classified Documents Expose Grim Reality of Comet Impact."

Pandemonium erupted on social media platforms, the voices of the citizens amalgamating into a chorus of disbelief, anger, and indignant calls for government accountability. Protests erupted in cities and towns, people wielding signs decrying the lies, the cover-ups, the calculated manipulation of facts that had kept them oblivious to the calamity racing toward Earth.

As Elaine watched the world react to the truths she had uncovered, her mind was a cyclone of conflicting emotions. Guilt wrestled with pride, anxiety skirmished with relief. Was this newfound transparency worth the inevitable chaos? Could she live with being the fulcrum of such seismic shifts in public sentiment and behavior? A momentary glance at her encrypted tablet revealed an anonymous message: "Thank you for your courage." A nanosecond of warmth crept into her veins, swiftly quenched by the ice-cold realization that her actions had also triggered an internal investigation within the government.

General Samuel Thompson, a man of imposing build and a face etched with years of military discipline, became the de facto inquisitor. His eyes, like cold blue steel, surveyed the members of the council, searching for signs of duplicity. He spoke, each word carefully weighted, "There's a traitor in our midst. Rest assured, the guilty party will be ferreted out and subjected to full military and civil prosecution." Elaine felt his gaze pierce through her, but whether he suspected her involvement was unclear.

Thompson had always been a guardian of governmental orthodoxy, a man who believed in the sanctity of the chain of command and the classified nature of national security information. As such, Elaine couldn't anticipate leniency from him if she were exposed. She had known Thompson for years, had sat across from him in numerous briefings and skirmishes of political gamesmanship. Yet now, he was an enigma, a formidable adversary in a game where the stakes were nothing less than the fate of the world.

As the hours passed in a haze of tension and speculation, Elaine received a cryptic message on her government-issued communication device. It was an invitation to a confidential meeting with General Thompson, the subject of which was not disclosed but implied a matter of utmost gravity. The coordinates pointed to a secluded chamber within the labyrinthine bunker, a place not marked on the official floorplans. Elaine felt a cascade of adrenaline flood her system. Her decision, a mingling of trepidation and resolve, was to attend the meeting.

With each step toward the unknown, Elaine's mind raced. Had her gambit been discovered? Was this confidential meeting a clandestine court-martial or something even more sinister? And if her identity as the whistleblower had indeed been unearthed, what could she possibly say in her defense?

The door to the chamber loomed before her, a monolithic slab of reinforced metal. She took a deep breath and entered her security code. The door yielded with a hydraulic hiss, revealing a dimly lit room. In the center stood General Thompson, his visage stern but his eyes betraying a flicker of something she couldn't quite place—was it animosity or something far more complex?

"Senator Mathews, please have a seat," he gestured to an unadorned metal chair opposite his own. "We have a lot to discuss."

CHAPTER 15: CONSEQUENCES AND REVELATION

Elaine eased into the chair, her eyes locked onto General Thompson's. There was something electric in the atmosphere, a tension that buzzed in the undercurrents of the room's muted air.

"Senator, the information leak has caused considerable unrest. You're aware of that, I assume?" Thompson began, his voice neither accusatory nor sympathetic.

Elaine nodded, her mind racing. "General, I won't play coy. We both know why I'm here. The question is, what happens now?"

A smile—subtle, almost imperceptible—flitted across Thompson's face. "I must say, I expected nothing less from you, Senator. You've always been one for directness."

Elaine clenched her fists under the table. She had anticipated various outcomes from this conversation: a confrontation, possible arrest, or even an unceremonious end to her political career. What she hadn't expected was Thompson's next words.

"Senator, you've actually done us a favor. Believe it or not, I'm not here to vilify you. In fact, I think the public deserved to know. The method, however, is where you and I differ."

Elaine's eyebrows shot up, her preconceived notions of Thompson dissipating like mist under the sun. "You're not opposed to the leak?"

"I believe in controlled transparency," Thompson clarified. "We're living on borrowed time, Senator. The old machinations of politics and military secrecy, while useful in a stable world, aren't worth a damn when a comet is on its way to erase us. But you went about it like a rogue elephant—trampling through sensitive terrain without regard for the aftermath."

Elaine listened intently, each of Thompson's words etching themselves into her consciousness. It was an unexpected pivot, an unforeseen alignment of views she had never thought possible.

"So what now?" Elaine asked cautiously, unsure of the ground she was treading.

Thompson leaned back, folding his arms. "A group of us within the government have been lobbying for more open disclosure about the comet. We're planning a calculated release of information, updates on preparations, and an honest portrayal of the odds we face."

"So, an institutionalized version of my leak?" Elaine interjected.

"In essence, yes," Thompson confirmed. "We're aiming for a level of transparency that can preserve social order while satisfying the public's right to know. But for this, Senator, we could use someone like you—a masterful political operator with the public's ear and a newfound ethical pivot."

It was decision time for Elaine. On the one hand, joining this faction within the government could serve as her lifeboat, a way out of potential disgrace and legal consequences. On the other hand, would she be sacrificing her ability to act unilaterally for what she deemed right?

Thompson seemed to sense her indecision. "I know it's a lot to take in, Senator. But consider this: You have already shifted the public discourse, forcing even those who would prefer continued secrecy to reconsider. You can be a part of this new phase. You could shape it. You would be a valuable asset and, in the days to come, I'd rather have another asset at my disposal than waste everyone's time and energy locking you up."

Elaine looked at Thompson, her eyes scanning his face for any sign of duplicity. She found none. After moments that felt like epochs, she finally spoke. "Alright, General. I'll join your group, work toward this 'controlled transparency' as you call it. But," she paused, choosing her words carefully, "I do this as an equal, not a subordinate. My maneuvers will be my own, even if they align with your objectives."

Thompson rose from his seat, extending his hand. "Agreed, Senator. This could very well be the genesis of a new era for government transparency – if anyone survives to remember it. Either way, we have work to do."

Elaine shook his hand, the gravity of her decision sinking in. As she walked through the labyrinthine halls back to the main council room, Elaine couldn't help but wonder if this, perhaps, was how legacies were forged—in clandestine meetings, under the looming shadow of cosmic oblivion, when individuals, regardless of their past, chose to redefine not just their own destinies, but that of a world standing on the precipice.

She was still a linchpin in the intricate machine of politics, but now, she had the potential to be a linchpin for change. It was a realization both sobering and exhilarating—as if, for the first time in her political career, she was part of a mechanism aimed at something genuinely constructive. She had moved from being a master of machinations to becoming a catalyst for something profoundly different.

And so, back in the council room, among men and women engrossed in their screens and data, Elaine felt a flicker of something rare and precious—hope. Not the naive hope that the comet would miraculously veer off course, but the hope that, in humanity's last days, the final chapters of their collective story could be written with a measure of dignity, honesty, and yes, transparency.

QUANTUM LOVE

CHAPTER 16: THE CODE OF AFFECTION

In a cavernous room resonating with the almost musical hum of servers and cooling units, Lena adjusted the lens of her microscope. Superconducting circuits embedded with qubits were at the heart of their last-ditch effort to avert cosmic calamity. The starkly lit lab seemed to buzz with an atmosphere heavy with both inspiration and desperation. Her eyes flicked to the holographic clock; it was far later than she had anticipated.

"Another all-nighter, Lena?" The voice belonged to Martin, her colleague, whose appearance bore the same weary markers— untidy hair, dark circles under his eyes. "We're close to something, aren't we?"

Lena sighed. "We're closer to annihilation every second, and yes, we might be on the edge of a solution—or another spectacular failure." She unclamped her eyes from the microscope and stared at the quantum computer core, its eerie light gleaming like the heart of some celestial object. "But time is a luxury, and it's running out."

Martin nodded. "I know. But we're doing everything humanly possible." His gaze met hers, searching for reassurance. "If quantum algorithms can provide us the computational power to alter that comet's trajectory, then—"

His sentence was interrupted by Lena's phone vibrating violently against the table. The ID displayed her husband's care facility. With an urgency that belied her calm demeanor, she grabbed the phone and walked into a quiet corner. The nurse's words were a litany of clinical jargon, but Lena distilled the essence: her husband's condition was deteriorating rapidly.

"Do you need to leave?" Martin's question, though couched in understanding, had a subtext she couldn't ignore—the tension between personal tragedy and the imminent end of the world.

She looked at her phone, her finger hovering over the call-back icon, and then slowly put it down. "No, I'm staying. What I'm doing here could impact millions, billions. John would understand. He always does."

As midnight approached, Lena found herself alone in the lab, the computer screens awash with incomprehensible data and algorithmic sequences. She couldn't shake off the thought of her husband lying in a sterile room, perhaps aware, in his own way, that their remaining time was dwindling just as rapidly as that of the planet. What a cruel game of probabilities life had turned out to be.

With a sudden, almost whimsical resolve, she navigated through the code she was working on—a quantum algorithm that, if successful, would pinpoint the precise calculations needed to deflect the comet. Before initiating the program, she typed a series of characters into a comment line, a sequence only she would understand. It was a simple message, "I love you, John, always," encoded in ASCII.

She leaned back as the quantum computer began processing the calculations, the qubits dancing in superposition, a ballet of zeros and ones, possibilities and certainties. But for Lena, it wasn't just about solving a cosmic problem. She had woven into the very fabric of this quantum challenge a deeply personal, human element—her love for her husband. It seemed to her then that love, like quantum information, was never really destroyed; it only changed states, manifested in different ways.

Minutes or eons passed—time seemed a blur. Finally, the screen displayed a series of numbers and graphs; the algorithm had run its course. But Lena was focused on something else, her own coded words hidden within, a subtext beneath the hard data. To any other eye, it was just another line of comment in a complex program, but to her, it was a quantum of her soul, a declaration of love entangled in the very computations that could determine the fate of Earth.

In that moment, in that sprawling temple of science, Lena felt infinitesimally small and yet boundlessly expansive. Here she was, a scientist driven by logic and empirical data, finding solace in an emotional abstraction. As she pondered this duality, she couldn't help but marvel at the complexity of human emotions, forever existing in a state of flux, much like the quantum bits she had just manipulated. She sat alone, among cables and glowing screens, embracing the ambiguity, comforted by the thought that in some parallel universe, maybe love was the key that solved every equation.

CHAPTER 17:
ENTANGLED HEARTS

Entangled in an emotional haze, Lena stepped away from the group of colleagues who'd congregated around the display monitors, their faces glowing in the artificial light. They were close; the algorithm she had fed into the quantum computer showed anomalies—fluctuations that teased at the fringes of theoretical possibility. Could this breakthrough be the one to divert the impending comet? A chorus of speculative conversations erupted, technical lexicons flying through the air like tangible equations.

Yet, the tone of hope in their discussion seemed almost cacophonous to Lena, jarring against the silent background of her internal world. She felt her phone vibrate softly in her pocket and instinctively knew who it was. Ignoring her colleagues' engrossing conversation about qubits and probabilities, she reached into her pocket and pulled out the phone.

The screen displayed a new message from John, timestamped just minutes ago. It was a simple text, but each word hit her like a particle wave, both illuminating and disorienting: "I love you, Lena. Succeed, for both of us."

John's words, despite their earnestness, deepened her emotional entanglement. A strange sense of duality swept over her. On one hand, there was her work—the labyrinth of equations and quantum states that could, in theory, save humanity. On the other, there was John—her constant, her variable, the love of her life now succumbing to an inoperable condition that no algorithm could solve. Two disparate worlds, seemingly unbridgeable, and yet inexorably tied to the core of her existence.

Drawing an uneven breath, Lena returned to her workstation. The quantum computer before her hummed softly, oblivious to her emotional maelstrom but intimately connected to the scientific endeavor she was part of. It struck her then: quantum entanglement, that peculiar phenomenon where particles become interconnected and the state of one instantly influences the state of another, no matter the distance separating them.

If particles could be so eternally entangled, couldn't her love for John? No-one else knew that she had taken to encoding simple ASCII text that conveyed John's messages to her and responses, their profound connection, within the folds of her groundbreaking research. In theory, it was irrelevant to the project. To Lena, these short messages felt like a statement about the purpose of her work.

With a newfound purpose, Lena resumed her work on the quantum algorithm. It was a complex lattice of equations, designed to manipulate the probabilities of quantum states. But nestled within this mathematical weave, Lena added something unquantifiable—a series of numbers that translated into an ASCII text, a message to John, hidden yet inseparable from the code: "Eternally entangled, my love."

It was a love letter woven into the very fabric of her most meaningful work, an indelible testament to their emotional entanglement. With a few final keystrokes, Lena embedded the personalized sequence into the algorithm and activated the quantum computation.

As the computer whirred to life, executing her revised algorithm, Lena felt a momentary connection with something beyond her own existence. If their impending doom were the result of cosmic indifference, then this—this entanglement of love and science— was her personal rebellion against the uncaring universe.

The quantum computer's visual monitor flickered, then displayed a series of outcomes. Probabilities shifted, some variables oscillating more wildly than before. Her colleagues would undoubtedly pore over this new data, looking for a key to humanity's survival. But whatever they found, Lena had already unlocked something unique—a love forever entangled in the intricacies of quantum mechanics.

Her phone vibrated again. Another message from John: "I'm proud of you, Lena. Always."

Whether her work would change the world or not remained uncertain, as did John's rapidly narrowing future. But as she stood there, cellphone in hand and staring at the cryptic quantum readouts, Lena realized that some entanglements—those of the heart—transcended both time and space, woven into the very fabric of her existence. And perhaps, in some unexplored corner of the quantum realm, that was enough.

CHAPTER 18: SINGULARITY

As Lena reentered the lab, the air seemed to crackle with a different kind of energy, as if the quantum computer itself had become sentient and was aware of the impending doom of Earth. Or perhaps it was simply the anxiety that pulsed through Lena's veins, magnified by the walls crammed with incomprehensible diagrams and matrices.

Her phone buzzed. She took a deep breath before she picked it up; it was a call from her husband's care facility. Without any prelude, the nurse on the other end delivered the news. John had passed away.

The air seemed to grow denser, each inhalation more laborious than the last. The news delivered a cognitive dissonance. She felt a chasm between her emotional turmoil and the urgency that still loomed like an unyielding monolith—her work was not yet done. The comet was still hurtling toward Earth.

Colleagues had already gathered around the central screen, excited murmurs filling the space.

"What's happening?" asked Lena confused.

"The latest results have come through. Lena, your algorithm—it worked. The quantum calculations, they've pinpointed a method to change the comet's trajectory," Martin said, waving her over to look at the screen. He sighed and shook his head, "Unfortunately, I've just had word from NASA and the White House that we are past the point of being able to implement it."

The data was conclusive; the models were almost unbelievably precise. Her algorithm would have worked. It could have been used to save humanity. Yet the time required for implementation eclipsed what was available. In the end, their breakthrough was a tragic exercise in cosmic irony: the solution was right there, materialized in strings of code and patterns of data, but time—the immutable, relentless force—had rendered it useless.

"Your code... it could have changed the fate of the world," Martin added, as if the words could offer any solace.

Lena felt the words pull at her, but they failed to anchor her drifting thoughts. She offered a muted nod, her eyes tracing the outline of her handwritten love message still displayed on a separate screen, like a poem lost in a sea of science.

"I have to go," she announced, grabbing her coat. "There's somewhere I need to be."

Leaving behind the room full of futile heroics, she walked toward the quantum computer. For a fleeting moment, she stared into its glowing core, its quantum bits entangled in states of uncertainty. To Lena, it appeared to flicker in a nuanced pattern, a subtle dance of light that seemed to echo the melody of her hidden message. It was as if the machine had transcoded her words into a language beyond human comprehension, into a symphony of quantum states. She couldn't be sure, of course. Science had no metric for such whimsical thoughts, and yet, she chose to believe it.

With a final glance, she keyed in the commands to lock down the lab. As she left, the quantum computer hummed back to life, running her algorithm one final time in a never-ending cycle. Her love message was now an indelible part of the calculations, woven into the strings of data that symbolized humanity's failed yet awe-inspiring effort to control its own destiny.

As she walked through the deserted corridors, her footsteps seemed to reverberate off the walls, each echoing step mirroring the duality she felt—a scientist who had almost rewritten the celestial script, a wife who could not be there in her husband's final moments.

Her work would go down in history, archived in data banks or perhaps even sent off into space for other civilizations to decipher. It would be a tribute not just to human ingenuity, but to love, loss, and the uncanny ability of the human spirit to find connections in the vast, indifferent arithmetic of the universe. And that connection, that transcendent unifying thread, was now saved in the form of quantum equations, a perfect marriage of numbers and emotions.

As Lena exited the building, the sky above displayed an array of colors, a beautiful dusk masking the havoc that was soon to follow. She realized that love, much like the mysterious laws governing the subatomic world, was a field of boundless potentialities. It was both tangible and elusive, a measurable constant yet also an unfathomable variable. And as she drove away, leaving behind the lab, the quantum computer, and fragments of her own heart, she sensed that love's elusive quantum state had been captured, if only momentarily, in the circuits and algorithms she had left behind. The calculations continued to hum in the empty lab, a requiem for a world on the brink, a lullaby for the love that once was and, in the fabric of spacetime, would always be.

ECHOES IN TIME

CHAPTER 19: THE DUST OF TOMES

Elizabeth's fingertips glided over the aged spines of books, each one a sentinel guarding the wisdom of centuries past. Her library, a cathedral of ancient texts and manuscripts, had always served as her sanctuary. Time seemed to halt among the wooden bookshelves and the intricate tapestries that adorned the walls. Outside, the world had descended into a whirlpool of pandemonium with the impending comet strike, but within these walls, a hallowed tranquility reigned.

Her phone buzzed on her desk, disrupting the stillness. The screen displayed her sister's name. Elizabeth sighed, picked it up, and braced herself.

"Beth, you need to leave now. This place won't survive the impact!" her sister's voice came through, tinged with hysteria.

"I can't, Sarah," Elizabeth said softly, her voice echoing her internal fortitude.

"Can't or won't?"

"There are things here, precious things that need to be preserved."

"They're just books, Beth!"

"To you, maybe. To me, they are the memory of our species. The echo of every man and woman who discovered something worth sharing."

Sarah fell silent, and Elizabeth took it as her cue to end the call. Setting the phone back on the table, her eyes fell upon an obscure, leather-bound manuscript penned by Phineas H. Warden, a largely forgotten philosopher who specialized in the ethics of survival during cosmic catastrophes. It had been an odd area of study at the time, but now, with the celestial menace drawing nearer each day, its relevance was undeniable.

She weighed the book in her hands. It was not particularly famous, nor had it been referenced in academic papers for decades. Yet, something about its aged pages called out to her. With a sense of sudden urgency, Elizabeth resolved to digitize it. She was not a technophile by any means, but she understood the significance of making this text accessible for whatever remnant of humanity might survive.

Taking great care, she moved to the scanning room. The process was slow and meticulous, requiring delicate handling to not damage the frail pages. As she worked, she felt the texture of the paper, the subtle imprints of ink, and thought about the hands that had originally written these words, the minds that had pondered them, and the mouths that had debated them. She was now, quite possibly, the last in that long lineage.

Just as she was halfway through the book, the lights flickered and went out. A pang of dread tightened her stomach. A power outage was the last thing she needed. She waited for a moment, her eyes straining in the darkness, and then with a defeated sigh, she felt her way back to the main hall to find the circuit board.

The moonlight that streamed through the gothic windows guided her to a closet where a backup generator was housed. Dusty but reliable, it had been a vestige from a bygone era of analog mechanisms. She cranked it to life, hoping it would last long enough for her to complete her task.

Returning to the scanning room, the dim light of the backup generator casting long shadows on the floor, she resumed her work. Each page scanned felt like a small victory against time and fate. She was now racing against the comet itself, each moment ticking away both universally and personally. If the wisdom within these pages was to have a ghost of a chance to survive, she had to continue.

As the scanner hummed, absorbing the archaic insights of Phineas H. Warden, Elizabeth considered her predicament. There were no guarantees that her efforts would amount to anything. There was no assurance that there would be anyone left to read these digital files or even equipment left to read them on. But the task provided her with a purpose, a flicker of meaning in the face of an otherwise random and capricious universe.

CHAPTER 20: THE FADING LIGHT

Elizabeth's eyes never left the scanner as it hummed, capturing the essence of each page, translating the philosopher's musings into bytes and pixels. The backup generator thrummed in the background, a lifeline to her race against time. As she maneuvered the fragile pages, her thoughts wandered, contemplating the infinite web of human history that lay within the walls of her cherished library.

Each tome, each manuscript, was a shout into the abyss of time, a desperate plea for remembrance. They were legacies of civilizations long gone, footprints in the cosmic sand. In this room alone were the accounts of ancient wars, treatises on social order, passionate love letters, and mathematical theorems that had been the zenith of human intellect in their respective eras. Even if humanity failed to avert this existential threat, even if her own life were but a blip in the continuum, these works could survive in digital form, echoing through the ages.

As the scanning machine worked its magic, the words of Phineas H. Warden resounded in her mind, instigating ripples of existential contemplation. His conjectures about humanity's instinct for survival in the face of cosmic disasters seemed eerily prescient. Did the historical records chronicled in these countless volumes justify the continuation of the human story? Had they learned enough, loved enough, destroyed enough, and created enough to warrant survival? These questions haunted her, but the philosopher offered no answers, only frameworks for thought.

Just as she was lost in her musings, the library's ancient wooden doors creaked open. Elizabeth looked up to see a group of disheveled people entering. It was a motley crew of refugees seeking sanctuary, clutching bundles and staring at the towering shelves as though they had entered another world.

"Miss, you should come with us. We're gathering at the town hall," a man at the front said, eyeing her warily.

"I appreciate the offer," Elizabeth replied, her gaze flicking back to the scanner. "But I have work to finish here."

"Work? Don't you know what's happening?" The man seemed incredulous.

"I know perfectly well," Elizabeth responded calmly. "But there are different forms of survival. I choose this."

The man hesitated, looked at his companions, and then nodded, his eyes filled with a strange mix of respect and confusion. The group shuffled back out, the door closing behind them with a sense of finality.

Elizabeth returned to the scanner, her fingers slightly trembling as she placed the last few pages on the glass surface. The machine whirred and clicked, signaling the end of its task. With a few more clicks, Elizabeth uploaded the digitized manuscript to the global archive, a network designed to survive almost anything, even a cataclysm of cosmic proportions. It was done. She had thrown her stone into the ocean of time, causing ripples that might one day wash ashore on a new world, in a new era, read by eyes that had never seen an Earthly dawn.

She sighed, a complex blend of relief, resignation, and fulfillment settling within her. Her eyes darted to the antique clock that adorned the wall. Time was running out. The comet, a celestial executioner, was making its final descent.

CHAPTER 21:
THE ECHO

Elizabeth sat back in her chair, regarding the scanning machine with a mixture of exhaustion and quiet triumph. The digital archives, now enriched with the obscure but prescient insights of Phineas H. Warden, offered her a momentary pause to reflect on the bigger picture. The room seemed to pulse around her, each book emanating its own story, its own unique blend of wisdom and folly. This was her life's work, her sacred duty—preserving the memory of the ages.

Compelled by an almost reverential desire, she stood up and began to wander through the labyrinthine stacks of the library. Her fingers lightly touched the worn spines of the books, each one a tactile connection to a past that was about to be irrevocably severed. The library had been her world, and as she moved through it, memories ebbed and flowed. Every section she passed —history, philosophy, science, literature—evoked a different era of her life. She had been a custodian of knowledge, and as she walked, she felt an overwhelming sense of both satisfaction and resignation.

At the far end of one aisle, a volume caught her eye—its faded leather cover almost hidden by the surrounding works. She took it down, her fingers trembling as she read the title: "The Eternal Echo," a philosophical work pondering the cyclical nature of history and society. She had never read this one, lost as it was among the library's rich collection. She opened it and began to read a passage that discussed the resilience of knowledge—the ways in which even as societies rise and fall, the echo of their existence, their discoveries, and their mistakes endures in the records they leave behind. The text seemed to reflect her own sentiments, her own hopes for the work she'd done.

She felt strangely connected to the author, as if the inked words were a bridge across time. The lines she read seemed to echo her recent thoughts and experiences in an almost eerie synchronicity. It was as if time had folded in upon itself, blurring the lines between the past and the present, the writer and the reader. The walls of the library seemed to close in around her, not oppressively, but like an embrace from the collective consciousness of humanity's long, fraught journey.

Before she could delve deeper, the ground beneath her feet shuddered. It was a low, grumbling tremor that resonated through the wooden floor and up the towering bookshelves. Dust shook loose from the ancient tomes; the air grew dense with the smell of aged paper and ink. The tremor intensified into a roar —distant yet omnipresent, as if the Earth itself were groaning in anticipation.

The comet was coming. The climax of human history, the curtain call for Earth's grand, chaotic theater, was but moments away.

Elizabeth took a deep breath and carefully returned the book to its place. She made her way back to her desk, where she had spent countless hours cataloging, researching, and cherishing the innumerable works that surrounded her. Her chair seemed to welcome her as she sat down, her eyes taking in the room—one final sweeping gaze at her life's passion.

It was then that a thought washed over her—a realization simple yet profound. She, like the authors of every book in this library, would become another echo in the corridors of time. Her efforts, her dedication to preservation, had perhaps ensured that somewhere down the line, someone might hear that echo, however faint. And wasn't that a form of immortality? A humble yet enduring legacy that transcended the transient nature of human existence?

A cacophony of noise, distant but rapidly approaching, began to fill the air. She knew it was time. Closing her eyes, Elizabeth rested her hands on her lap. Amidst the grand wealth of human thought that filled the room, she found herself oddly at peace, ready to add her own whisper to the unending dialogue between the past and whatever future might remain. An echo that would reverberate long after the noise had faded into an eternal, cosmic silence.

NEON DESPAIR

CHAPTER 22:
PROPHECY

Jasper's feet whispered secrets to the cracked pavement, each step a clandestine symphony of urban disquiet. Draped in garments that had long since surrendered their original hue to the indistinct grays and browns of city life, he moved like a wraith through the maze of concrete and steel. It was a city lit by the ghostly glow of neon signs, where graffiti whispered tales of disillusionment across decaying walls, and shattered windows sang elegies of forgotten dreams.

But tonight, Jasper was on a quest, led by something both ephemeral and visceral—perhaps it was a murmur from the stars or an itch in the marrow of his bones. His worn notebook, a relic brimming with scribbled prophecies and revolutionary sketches, rested against his chest as he traversed the landscape. He passed the huddled forms of the homeless, burrowed into tattered sleeping bags as if they could tunnel away from the world's despair. Gang members loitered on corners, dealing fleeting pleasures wrapped in ephemeral dreams, as desolate as the space between atoms.

It was then that he saw her—Helen, her eyes vast pools of confusion. Dressed too thinly for the night's chill, her face carried the fragility of someone long misplaced in life's labyrinth. "Are you lost?" she asked, or maybe she was just thinking aloud.

Jasper hesitated, then fumbled to open his notebook. His hands flipped through pages filled with almost coherent visions and fragmented symbols. He showed her a recent entry—a sketch of a comet tail splayed across the night sky like cosmic brush strokes, its nucleus a radiant pearl.

"That's beautiful, but what does it mean?" Helen looked as if she was trying to catch wisps of hope, trying to contain them in the stark lines of his drawing. Absently she scratched the track marks along her arms and pulled her sleeve down to cover them.

"It's a prophecy," Jasper replied, his voice tinged with a mystic's fervor. "A vision of rebirth. The celestial paintbrush will cleanse the canvas. A fresh beginning, not an end. We don't have to be victims of annihilation; we can be children of transformation."

Helen glanced from the notebook to Jasper's earnest face, then back to the cruel city around them. "Do you really believe that? In a place like this?"

Jasper became agitated again, "I must. Otherwise, what's the point of dreaming?"

He led Helen to a stretch of wall that seemed less tainted than its neighbors, as if waiting for its destiny to be spray-painted into existence. Jasper removed a can of aerosol paint from his tattered rucksack, shaking it until its contained potential became an audible rattle—a chaotic dance of atoms yearning for release.

As he pressed the nozzle, celestial symbols and cosmic shapes emerged from the mist of paint, glowing eerily in the dim light. Encrypted constellations wove into messages only discernible to those fluent in the lexicon of despair and hope. For a few minutes, he was not merely Jasper, the street prophet in a decaying world, but a herald of possibilities, a conjurer of hidden universes.

Finally, he stepped back, the last spray of paint adding a comet that seemed to burst from the wall, its tail almost tangible in the ghostly glow of a nearby neon sign. It was as if he'd created a rift in the fabric of reality, a secret door through which one could glimpse another outcome for humanity.

"What do you think?" Jasper turned to Helen, who was watching, mesmerized by the act of creation she had just witnessed.

"It's... miraculous," she breathed, dreamily. "For a moment, I forgot where we are."

Jasper nodded. "That's the point. In every message of doom, there's an embedded cipher of salvation. You just need to know how to look. It's deep, but it's there." He tapped the side of his head rapidly as if to demonstrate. Sarah smiled blankly and then returned her attention to the mural.

As he packed his rucksack, Helen took a photograph of the graffiti with her cracked phone. "I want to remember this," she said, "especially if you're right about what comes next."

Jasper knew that the comet, visible now even in the blaze of the city's artificial light, would either vindicate or obliterate his visions soon enough. As they parted ways, each moving like celestial bodies bound to different orbits, he looked back at his graffiti. Amidst the rust and ruin, it stood as a cryptic message, a paradox of dread and hope, waiting to be deciphered by souls brave or desperate enough to believe in its ambivalent promise.

CHAPTER 23: TAG

Jasper lingered before the graffiti he had just rendered on the decaying wall—an enigmatic blend of symbols and celestial forms, a riddle encoded in aerosol pigments. The city sprawled before him, a lumbering behemoth of urban decay. Towers of concrete and steel loomed like lifeless titans, windows vacant as a dead man's eyes. Neon lights flickered sporadically, veins of false vitality in an otherwise moribund metropolis. Each sign, every glaring billboard, seemed a mockery, a hideous grin on the face of impending calamity. It was a dystopia created from the fabric of despair—a world undone, staggering under the weight of its own failed aspirations.

For a fleeting moment, he was transported back to a different time. A memory wafted into his consciousness, unbidden yet desperately needed. He had once been a promising artist, armed with nothing but a collection of hopeful sketches and an unassailable dream. He recalled the gleaming city as it used to be, not a wasteland but a sprawling canvas, each skyscraper a monument to human achievement. How distant those days seemed, how naively idyllic. The echo of that earlier life clashed with his present reality, forming a dissonant chord that tugged at the vestiges of his sanity.

As he shook off the haunting reverie and prepared to move deeper into the urban labyrinth, a new sound broke through the ambient cacophony of sirens, car horns, and distant, unintelligible shouting—a voice, authoritative yet tinged with the unmistakable tone of weary apathy. A police officer, uniform neglected and stained, emerged from the spectral mist created by a nearby streetlight.

"Hey, you! What do you think you're doing?" The words carried more resignation than inquiry.

Jasper met the officer's eyes, finding there not the fire of duty but the dim flicker of someone who had seen the social contract erode beneath his feet. Both men paused, a tableau framed by the surrounding disarray. The officer glanced at Jasper's spray cans, then back to the cryptic mural on the wall. A sigh escaped his lips, replacing the question he seemed to decide was not worth asking.

"Just move along, would you?" the officer finally muttered, embodying the erosion of institutional authority in a city spiraling into oblivion.

Jasper nodded, not in deference but in mutual understanding of the ineffable tragedy that enveloped them both. Slipping past the officer, he discreetly left another tag on the corroded surface of a metal trash bin—an emblem of a comet, racing across an implied sky.

Jasper left the scene, vanishing into the labyrinthine backstreets, but not before casting one last, lingering gaze upon the world he knew. It was a realm suspended between creation and ruin, an elegy scrawled in the medium of urban decay. Yet, in its dismal visage, he saw a canvas. It was a surface upon which messages could be scratched, cries for understanding, or maybe— just maybe—tokens of hope amid the impending cosmic finale.

Jasper may not have had the tools to stop the comet, but he had the means to communicate, to leave an indelible mark upon the world's final days. And in the existential arithmetic of life's last moments, that small increment was not just something. It was everything.

CHAPTER 24: AWAKENINGS

Upon hearing the news of the confirmed comet impact, Jasper felt an eerie sense of vindication. Amidst the pervasive dread, a whisper of destiny beckoned him. He found himself in another dilapidated alley, encrusted with the detritus of human neglect. The walls around him were scarred with crude caricatures and vulgar exclamations, graffiti devoid of intent, artistic or otherwise. This was a corner of the world that had surrendered to entropy long before the celestial executioner was slated to arrive.

He reached into his rucksack and retrieved the cans of spray paint he had reserved for this precise moment of hopelessness — vivid hues of electric blue, luminous orange, and phosphorescent green. These were the colors of his final testament, his ultimate prophecy. With a frenzied focus that came from a place beyond mere skill, a place where inspiration and desperation intertwined, Jasper began to paint.

The result was an intricate image of the comet, encased in a halo of blazing light, surrounded by a labyrinth of cryptic symbols, equations, and questions without answers. Each curve of aerosol paint seemed a meditation on cosmic insignificance, each line a probe into the fabric of earthly despair. Yet, at the heart of this creation was a single word, a human word, glowing like a shard of light in the dark corridor: "Awaken."

Just as he was affixing the final touch to his opus, a familiar voice fractured the still air. Helen had returned, her eyes glowing with an intensity that Jasper hadn't observed before. She had seen his other pieces, she said, photographing each with her battered phone, investing each image with the reverence of a pilgrim collecting relics.

"You've given me something to do," she said, her words tinged with a nascent sense of purpose. "I haven't used since the last time we met. Instead, if I need to escape, I just lose myself in your images." She hesitated and then held out her phone, scrolling through the images, "I've been documenting them. Maybe they can live on in some form, beyond these walls."

Jasper looked up from his work, his eyes meeting Helen's. For the first time, he allowed himself the luxury of envisioning his graffiti existing beyond the lifespan of physical structures. As they stood there, the very air seemed charged with potentiality, an electric buzz that drowned out the dismal hum of the city.

"I think this is your masterpiece," Helen whispered, pointing at the newly finished graffiti. "It's as if you've condensed all the chaos, all the despair, into something coherent, something that beckons us to look deeper, to seek connections where we saw only randomness. It's beautiful."

Jasper took a step back, absorbing his creation as if for the first time. Despite the chaos around him, despite the impending comet, he felt a deep-rooted satisfaction.

"Would you like to take the last photo?" he offered, handing Helen a can of spray paint. "Add your touch. Make it a collaboration."

With a hint of hesitation, Helen took the can and added a simple but evocative swirl of color that spiraled out from the comet, as if charting its path through the cosmos.

As she stood back and held his hand, something strange and wondrous happened. The graffiti seemed to quiver, to shimmer with an energy of its own. For a split second, both Helen and Jasper felt as though they were peering through a veil into an alternate reality, one where humanity had succeeded in untangling the cosmic puzzle just in time. Then the moment passed, leaving them standing in the same run-down alley, surrounded by the same decaying city, with the same comet inexorably drawing closer.

The comet, now visible to the naked eye even amidst the urban light pollution, seemed to hang in the sky like an indictment. Yet, Jasper couldn't help but see it also as a confirmation, an affirmation of some absurd cosmic narrative.

As they walked away side by side, each felt the weight of the finality that the universe had imposed. Yet, both carried with them an inexplicable sense of hope, or if not hope, at least meaning. Their graffiti had achieved something sublime, something that transcended the individual and aspired to the universal. It had become more than paint on a wall; it was a mysterious sign, a piece of the larger cosmic puzzle that humanity was racing to understand. And in that enigmatic swirl of color and symbol, two lost souls had found, if not salvation, then a glimmer of something eternal.

COSMIC DUST

CHAPTER 25:
VANTAGE POINT

Captain Mark Harper, ensconced in the sterile ambiance of the international satellite's command module, scrutinized the screen before him. The equations, trajectory vectors, and simulations seemed unreal—mathematical nightmares, dispassionate yet irrevocable in their implications. He double-checked the variables, revisited the assumptions, and verified the constraints. When the system returned the same outcome, a disquieting certainty gripped him. The comet was coming, and its collision with Earth was inescapable.

He activated the communication panel. "Mission Control, this is Commander Harper. Requesting a re-confirmation of data set alpha-seven regarding the incoming object."

The response was uncharacteristically tardy. Eventually, a voice crackled through the static. "Commander Harper, Mission Control here. We've run the numbers multiple times. I'm afraid the conclusions are consistent with your findings. Impact is imminent."

"Understood," Mark whispered, severing the connection.

He swiveled his chair toward the observation window, staring at the planet below. How many times had he looked upon Earth from this orbital vantage point? He had witnessed the tumultuous swirls of hurricanes, the dazzling flash of lightning storms, the microscopic dance of ships and planes, and even the devastating blooms of battlefields. Each sight had infused him with a cocktail of emotions—awe, exhilaration, and at times, somber contemplation. Now, all these chaotic elements of humanity's theater seemed trivial, mere ephemeral sketches on the canvas of cosmic time.

From his early years, Mark had been fascinated by the stars, inspired by the pioneers who had ventured into the unknown. As a boy, he dreamt of interstellar journeys and distant galaxies, yearning to push humanity's frontier beyond the limits of imagination. He joined space programs, excelled in the rigors of astronaut training, and was eventually entrusted with commanding missions. In a different life, Mark could have been a Prometheus, stealing celestial secrets to light humanity's way. Now, it seemed he'd be more of an unwilling chronicler of its twilight.

The cruel paradox was that this disaster rendered all the cosmic beauty surrounding him both profoundly significant and woefully insignificant. The jewel-like Earth floated in a sea of darkness, as if nature itself was oblivious to the impending cataclysm. The forests would still stand tall, at least for a while, rivers would keep flowing, and the mountains would continue their stoic vigil until the very end. Yet, every flicker of human achievement, each monument and every verse, all of it would vanish, indistinguishable from the cosmic dust that predated the dawn of man.

Closing his eyes momentarily, Mark grappled with a decision. He could continue to mull over the existential questions that had no answers, or he could act within the limitations of his reality. Despite the cosmic curtain falling over human history, wasn't it his duty, as an astronaut and a scientist, to offer whatever he could?

Returning his attention to the console, Mark activated the recording system. Data, however disheartening, still needed to be communicated. His report wouldn't offer salvation, but it could provide perspective, an analytical lens through which to perceive the impending destruction. Even if the report proved futile for altering their fate, perhaps it could serve as a token of resistance, a final affirmation of human agency in the face of overwhelming cosmic indifference.

Switching to data-gathering mode, Mark Harper prepared to analyze whatever information he could obtain about the malevolent celestial body hurtling through space. It was a task tinged with despair, yet carried out with the kind of stoic resolve that had guided him throughout his career.

He didn't know it then, but this would be his last report to Earth, a testament that might give those on the doomed planet a last fragment to consider, a lingering thought to explore before the annihilation of everything they had ever known.

CHAPTER 26:
DUST DATA

Mark Harper toggled through screens filled with lines of data, graphs, and spectral readouts, each presenting a grim analysis of the approaching comet. Despite the staggering technology housed within the satellite, his efforts to find something—anything—that could avert the impending disaster felt increasingly quixotic. With each completed algorithm and verified data point, the insidious truth sank deeper: the comet was unstoppable, an astronomical juggernaut set on a collision course with Earth.

Yet he persisted, setting the satellite sensors to probe the comet's composition for volatile compounds or elemental quirks that could hint at a vulnerability. His mind wandered back to his family—his wife, Julia, and their two children. He imagined them in their suburban home, eyes glued to news reports, faces a mix of disbelief and fear. How would they face the end? Would they find comfort in each other's presence or would despair dominate their final days?

The computer chirped, pulling him back to the present. The sensors had finished collecting the latest round of spectral data. Mark scanned the results, his eyes moving rapidly over the lines of information. Nothing. The comet was a monolithic entity of ice, rock, and metals. No apparent weaknesses. No miraculous solutions.

Shutting down the data stream, he swiveled his chair and activated the satellite's high-resolution camera. Aimed at Earth, the camera captured stunning images of the planet—its vibrant blues, browns, and greens standing in stark contrast to the ink-black void of space. If these were to be among the last images of Earth, he would make sure they were flawless, a testament to the planet's fragile beauty.

Diverting from the scientific, Mark initiated a new document on his console, a textual attachment to accompany his report. It was not a task mandated by Mission Control, nor would it contain any groundbreaking discoveries. Instead, he would try to encapsulate the surreal experience of watching the world end from the unique perch of an orbiting satellite. The cursor blinked expectantly.

He began to type, each keystroke echoing in the chamber as he wrote of Earth's monumental insignificance in the cosmic scale, and yet, its irreplaceable value to the ones calling it home. Could the coexistence of both paltry insignificance and profound importance be the essence of human life? Each person a transient spark in the vast timeline of the universe, yet each life immeasurably significant to the people it touched?

With a sense of resigned tranquility, Mark concluded the attachment. He saved the document, appended it to his report, and sent the entire package hurtling through the digital ether back to Earth. As the transmission indicator blinked its affirmation, a semblance of peace settled over him. Whether his words would be read, whether they would matter at all, was uncertain. And yet, he felt a small but significant weight lift off his shoulders.

He leaned back in his chair, casting one final glance at the spectral data that had refused to offer humanity a lifeline. The irony wasn't lost on him. In seeking to examine the comet, to break it down to its base elements, he had ended up dissecting his own existence, breaking down the complexities of human life to its simple, dualistic nature—utterly inconsequential on a cosmic level, yet deeply significant on a human one.

Mark deactivated the screens and dimmed the lights, leaving only the soft glow from the observation window to fill the cabin. Outside, the celestial tapestry stretched infinitely, indifferent to the drama unfolding in the solar system. And somewhere in that sea of cosmic indifference, a speck of light marked the comet, growing brighter with each passing moment.

As he looked out into the abyss, waiting for the comet to make its final, fiery descent, he realized that even in the face of imminent annihilation, there existed room for acceptance, for peace, and perhaps, for a subtle but meaningful form of triumph.

CHAPTER 27: ODYSSEY

The communication panel blinked to life, flooding the dimly lit satellite cabin with a cascade of soft light. "Commander Harper, this is Mission Control," the voice came through with a clarity that belied the unfathomable distance it had traveled. "Your data has been received. It's invaluable and will form part of the intelligence for Project Odyssey —the final mission to preserve something of humanity. Thank you."

Mark Harper sighed, his eyes drifting to the Earth below him. Floating within the celestial vastness, its blues and greens punctuated by swirling whites, it resembled less a sturdy, steadfast planet and more a fragile orb—a droplet in the cosmic ocean, soon to vanish in a scalding blaze.

Pressing a button, Mark activated the satellite's live broadcasting system. It was a feature intended for educational outreach programs, for sharing the wonders of space science with eager students back on Earth. Today, it would serve a different purpose.

"Hello, Earth," he began, his voice calm and steady. "This is Captain Mark Harper, aboard the International Observation Satellite. If you're hearing this, it's likely one of the last broadcasts you'll receive from space."

He paused, choosing his words with the sort of meticulous care that had been drummed into him during his astronaut training, but which now seemed laughably irrelevant. "By now, you've heard about the comet. You know that it's unstoppable, and that our collective time is limited. This reality is inescapable, even from my vantage point here in space."

Mark leaned back, peering into the camera. "And yet, from this vantage point, you gain a certain clarity. It's easy to see how small we are in the grand scheme of things. The universe doesn't care about us; we're mere specks of cosmic dust on a slightly larger speck, orbiting an unremarkable star in an indifferent galaxy."

For a moment, the weight of what he was saying struck him, and his voice faltered. "However, in this fleeting moment we call existence, we have the ability to make it meaningful. Our lives are complex, fraught with love and despair, filled with moments of elation and times of sorrow. And in this complexity, in our relationships and achievements, we find significance. We find purpose."

His eyes drifted to the Earth again, its splendor almost too painful to behold. "So as the end approaches, don't think about what could have been. Don't dwell on the insignificance of it all. Instead, think about what still can be, in these final days or hours. Hold your loved ones. Speak your truth. Make peace where you can."

He leaned forward, his eyes locked on the camera. "Go out embracing the paradox that is human life: both trivial and profoundly meaningful. And know that while the universe may not care, you have the capacity to care immensely—and that makes all the difference."

Mark switched off the broadcasting system, his heart pounding in his chest as he processed what he'd just done. As if in response, a dash of light caught his eye—brighter than before, and unmistakably closer. The comet was approaching, visible even from his orbital height.

He unbuckled his safety harness and pushed gently against the floor, propelling himself across the cabin towards the observation window. His floating form came to rest against the glass, face to face with his home planet, its silent beauty marred by the glowing harbinger of its demise.

For a long time, he just stared, his thoughts dissipating into the wordless depth of his emotions. Here, the cosmic dance was stripped down to its most essential components: a planet, a comet, and a lone observer suspended between the two.

Finally, he spoke, whispering as though fearful of breaking the sacred silence of space. "Goodbye, Earth. Goodbye, my loves. You were my world, and for a moment, that was enough."

Mark's gaze lingered on the approaching comet, the growing brightness etching a vivid, indelible impression on his retinas. As his breathing slowed, he pondered the two contradictory truths that had come to define his final days: the irrelevance and the enormity of it all. And in that moment, poised on the edge of oblivion, he felt the walls between them crumble, leaving only the simple, aching beauty of a world—and a life— about to end. Whether he'd live to see the impact or not became inconsequential; he had reconciled his existence within the grand indifference of the cosmos, finding a moment of purpose, of poignant significance, even as the curtains closed.

And so, Mark Harper, astronaut and unlikely philosopher, floated in the eternal night, a lone observer to the closing act of the human drama, as a tear drifted from his eye, glittering like a transient star before being swallowed by the void.

BIOLOGICAL CLOCK

CHAPTER 28: THE DEEP FOREST

Dr. Evelyn Harmon brushed aside an errant vine, her eyes scanning the lush forest that stretched endlessly in every direction. It was a pristine sanctuary, a hidden gem tucked away in a remote corner of the planet. Here, life flourished in its most unspoiled form, a vivid tapestry of biodiversity. For a person like Evelyn, whose life was committed to the documentation and study of Earth's ecosystems, this forest was a holy grail of scientific endeavor.

Time, a dimension that humankind had sought to measure and control, seemed to blur in this idyllic setting. The forest was a chronicle of evolutionary artistry, its dense canopies and underbrush harboring secrets yet untold. However, despite the air of timelessness that hovered around her, Dr. Harmon couldn't escape the gnawing reality that the celestial hourglass was almost empty. The comet, a harbinger of global cataclysm, had punctured the comforting illusion of human permanence. News reports, once filled with a mixture of denial and hope, had now coalesced into a grim acceptance.

Evelyn paused, her boots sinking into the moist earth. She reflected on the path that had brought her here, to this remote Eden. While her peers had chosen more conventional settings for their lives—laboratories with controlled variables, universities with burgeoning young minds—Evelyn had chosen the unpredictability of the wilderness. A choice made easier, perhaps, by the lack of close family or romantic entanglements. She had spent her life cataloging the natural world, adding layers of understanding to the intricate web that composed life on Earth. To many, her work seemed to be an obscure curiosity, but to Evelyn, it was a life of purpose, a quest for truth in its most unadulterated form.

As she navigated through a particularly dense thicket, her keen eyes caught an anomaly: an oddly shaped footprint imprinted on a patch of mud. She knelt down, her fingers tracing the irregular outline. It wasn't the track of any species she recognized, and the forest had been her silent companion long enough for her to claim such expertise. Intrigued, she moved forward, her senses heightened. More signs became apparent—a displacement of foliage here, an unusual scattering of droppings there, even the subtle alteration in the scent of the forest air.

Each clue whispered promises of a hitherto unknown life form, an undiscovered species that had managed to escape human scrutiny. In that moment, the significance of this potential discovery unfurled before her like a cosmic tapestry. If she could find this creature, document it, she could immortalize a tiny yet irreplaceable fragment of Earth's biological diversity. With every step, her conviction strengthened. Here was a living, breathing entity, a being whose existence was a thread in the ecological tapestry, a note in the symphony of life.

Evelyn knew she was against the clock, racing not just against the setting sun but against the inexorable approach of the comet. Yet, the urgency of her own finite timeline seemed to fuel rather than hinder her determination. Here was her purpose distilled into a single quest, a microcosm of her lifelong commitment to Earth's biodiversity. Her work had often felt like an act of resistance against human neglect and hubris. Now, as the hours dwindled to minutes, as weeks shrank to days, she recognized that her work could serve as an act of affirmation—an ode to life on the planet she loved so deeply.

With resolute eyes, Dr. Evelyn Harmon readied her field kit. It was a humble collection of tools—a handheld GPS, a compact digital camera, a notebook filled with hastily scrawled observations—but in her skilled hands, they were instruments of revelation. Even if the world was standing on the precipice of oblivion, she would pursue this discovery with the zeal that had characterized her entire career. After all, even as the shadow of extinction loomed large, here was a possibility, however faint, of capturing and preserving a slice of Earth's magnificent, often overlooked, biological richness.

Evelyn breathed in deeply, absorbing the forest's rich, earthy aroma. She would venture deeper into the woods, leaving no stone unturned in her quest for this elusive creature. For her, it was not just a matter of scientific inquiry but a form of spiritual sustenance. Even if the world was destined to end, she would spend her last days as she had lived her life—engaged in the ceaseless pursuit of knowledge, enraptured by the sublime complexity of Earth's living systems.

As the sun dipped below the horizon, casting its last golden rays through the towering trees, Dr. Evelyn Harmon moved forward. She would find this creature, she vowed silently. She would document this last unknown species, not as a swan song of despair but as a testament to the boundless wonders of the planet she called home. With her eyes set firmly ahead, she ventured deeper into the forest, a lone biologist on the cusp of an enigmatic world, guided by an unyielding love for the Earth and its mysteries.

CHAPTER 29: THE LAST UNKNOWN SPECIES

Dr. Evelyn Harmon sat in a makeshift tent, her eyes narrowed as she reviewed the footage captured by her strategically placed camera traps. Her laptop screen flickered with brief glimpses of the forest's denizens—anteaters, spiders, and various birds—each making their cameo before retreating back into the wilderness. But what Evelyn was looking for had eluded her so far: the enigmatic creature that had left behind those peculiar tracks and odd environmental markers. Her setup was extensive; she had used everything from camera traps to acoustic monitoring devices and environmental DNA sampling techniques.

Her meticulousness was an artifact of decades in scientific research, each step governed by a methodology crafted from both rigorous training and hard-won experience. Evelyn knew the perils of false positives, the folly of observer bias. Hence, her grid of equipment was carefully calibrated to account for variables like weather, time of day, and the idiosyncrasies of animal behavior. The slightest anomaly was probed, evaluated for statistical significance, and then either absorbed into the data set or discarded as noise.

Finally, as she was reviewing the latest batch of acoustic

recordings, she saw it—a fleeting figure caught on one of the camera traps. It was a small mammal, agile and well-adapted to its complex surroundings. Its fur bore an uncanny resemblance to the colors of the forest floor, and its eyes were keen, almost as if aware of the camera's prying gaze. Evelyn's heart leapt; the thrill of discovery, as intense as ever, flooded her senses.

She set about documenting her find with an almost ritualistic reverence. Each observed behavior, each physical characteristic was annotated, categorized, and cross-referenced with existing literature. It may not have possessed any remarkable features like bio-luminescence or novel biochemical compounds, but it was an unknown species nonetheless. And in the taxonomy of life on Earth, each new entry was invaluable.

Yet even as she worked through this rigorous process, a different set of emotions began to unfold within her. This was a eulogy as much as it was an epiphany. This creature, so finely adapted to its niche, would probably never see another generation. Its life strategy, evolved over countless millennia, would be rendered obsolete by a hunk of rock hurtling through space. The dispassionate scientist in her chafed at the sentimentality of it all, but the human being who had given her life to the study of Earth's biodiversity couldn't help but feel a profound sense of sorrow.

She uploaded her carefully annotated observations, the diagrams, and even the DNA sequences she'd managed to obtain, to a global scientific repository. A server farm located in a climate-controlled facility would dutifully store her data. Whether human eyes would ever scrutinize her research again was uncertain, but the action felt like planting a time capsule for a future that might never arrive. A message in a bottle thrown into an infinitely expanding cosmic ocean.

Yet, even amid this existential bleakness, Evelyn found an island of consolation. She had, in the waning moments of this world, added to the annals of human knowledge. The comet's apocalyptic descent may be inevitable, but so was the pull of human curiosity, the need to explore and document. She had fulfilled her role in that grand endeavor, just as every organism in this forest had fulfilled its role in the grand tapestry of life. It was a small victory, perhaps imperceptible against the backdrop of impending doom, yet deeply meaningful to her.

Dr. Harmon took a deep breath, her eyes moving away from the screen and focusing back on the forest outside her tent. It was as if each leaf, each droplet of rain, and each rustle of the wind carried a new resonance for her. This forest, like the new species she had just documented, might not have a tomorrow. But in that very transience, she found a strange and compelling sense of permanence. The Earth had seen countless dawns and dusks, and life had always found a way to persist. She couldn't say for sure what would happen after the comet struck, but she had made her peace with the uncertainty. After all, discovery was not just about finding something new, but also about learning to see the familiar with newfound awe.

CHAPTER 30: ARK

Dr. Evelyn Harmon was surrounded by a cocoon of organized chaos. Her research station, a makeshift tent that had been her sanctuary for months, now resembled a hive in the midst of abandonment. Scientific instruments, observational notebooks, and vials of biological samples were being systematically cataloged, each object a treasured relic from an era that was inching closer to its conclusion.

As she meticulously packed away her equipment, Evelyn's mind wandered like a butterfly through a garden of existential musings. She had always been fascinated by the cyclical phenomena in nature—the metamorphosis of a caterpillar into a butterfly, the rejuvenating rains that brought life to arid lands, even the grander cycles of glacial epochs and mass extinctions. Life on Earth was a colossal wheel, forever turning, forever seeking equilibrium. And she, a lone biologist cataloging the genetic scripts of a vanishing world, felt like a transient speck on the wheel's ever-spinning rim.

Her reflections led her to a place of profound philosophical contemplation. In the grand scheme of things, was this cosmic calamity—this comet hurtling toward Earth—merely another turn of the wheel? Planetary epochs had come and gone, each characterized by its unique assemblages of flora and fauna. Each catastrophic shift, whether induced by volcanic eruptions or asteroid impacts, had served as a reset button, after which life had adapted, evolved, and flourished anew.

Were she and her contemporaries, then, mere witnesses to yet another cyclical shift? A cataclysmic reshuffling of Earth's biological deck of cards? While the thought offered no comfort for the individual lives that would be extinguished, including her own, it did provide a strange sense of context. She felt her work, her very existence, dissolve into something much larger—a fleeting brushstroke in the Earth's epic, still-unfolding mural.

In the midst of her reverie, her eyes fell upon the communication console. A dusty screen and an array of switches sat there, a tenuous link to the world outside her forest enclave. With a resigned sigh, she walked over to shut it down, severing her last technological umbilical cord. Just as her finger hovered over the power switch, the screen blinked to life, startling her. A message notification flashed urgently.

The message was from a team of scientists, visionaries who were constructing humanity's last refuge: a space ark designed to be a self-sustaining biosphere. They had stumbled upon her data repository, particularly her documentation of the new species. Her heart swelled as she read further; they were interested in incorporating this species into the ark. According to their computational models, the creature's unique attributes—its adaptability, its ecological role—made it a linchpin species, one that could confer resilience and stability to a closed ecosystem.

It was a bolt from the blue, an unexpected turn in a narrative she had presumed was reaching its inexorable end. The message concluded with a sincere expression of gratitude and a sober acknowledgment: "We wish you could join us, Dr. Harmon. Your work will, in a very real sense, live on."

Evelyn leaned back in her chair, overwhelmed. Her pulse quickened not from the dread of impending annihilation but from an upswell of unforeseen hope. No, she would not witness the next chapter of life's ever-unfolding saga, but she could contribute to it. That her life's work might form a vital building block in the continued story of Earth's biodiversity filled her with a profound sense of fulfillment, a gratification that transcended the moribund reality enveloping her.

With newfound serenity, Dr. Harmon stepped out of her tent. The sky was a dark canvas upon which the stars painted their ancient light. And there it was—the comet, a blazing harbinger no longer of doom but a celestial wayfarer ushering in the next epoch. As she stood there, her eyes skyward but her thoughts deeply rooted in the world around her, she understood the most intimate of paradoxes: life, in its ever-changing forms, persists through cycles of cataclysm and rebirth.

CODED

CHAPTER 31: THE IMPERATIVE CODE

Eleanor stared at her computer screen, lost in the labyrinthine world of code that sprawled across it. Her colleagues around her were similarly engrossed in their own digital microcosms, ostensibly insulated from the sense of urgency that permeated every molecule of air. In Eleanor's case, the code wasn't just a set of arbitrary instructions; it was a harbinger of evolution, a potential leap in artificial intelligence that carried enormous ethical weight. She was teetering on the brink of initiating a program that could allow her AI, Athena, to evolve and adapt even after humanity had succumbed to the inevitable catastrophe.

Years ago, Eleanor had embarked on the Athena project with the modest intention of creating an advanced decision-making engine for disaster relief. It had been her life's work, but as she refined its algorithms and enhanced its learning capabilities, she realized that she had endowed Athena with the potential for something far more profound. Could a machine assume a sort of stewardship over the remnants of civilization? Should it?

Ethical dilemmas gnawed at her. Giving a machine the ability to self-improve was one thing; doing so at the cusp of human extinction was another. As humanity's reign teetered on the edge, should its technological offspring be given the reins?

Eleanor's supervisor, Mr. Simmons, passed by her workstation, glancing cursorily at her screen. "Still wrestling with that algorithm, Eleanor? Remember, we only need it for basic disaster coordination."

"I'm aware, sir," she replied, forcing a smile. Simmons was not privy to the clandestine updates she had been injecting into Athena. Those updates were her own surreptitious addendums, born from a blend of curiosity, ambition, and a dash of existential despair.

Feeling the weight of her dilemma, Eleanor initiated a secure video call to her old mentor, Dr. Karen Holt. Karen's face flickered on the screen, a semblance of calm in a disquieting world. "Eleanor, it's been a while. To what do I owe the pleasure?"

"I'm facing an ethical dilemma, Karen. Normally I would have hundreds of discussions about this and get board approval but there just isn't time. With the comet coming, should I give Athena the ability to continue evolving? At this stage, it's a hail Mary, but I guess I figure, what do we have to lose?"

Karen sighed deeply. "The technology we create is a mirror to our ambitions and our fears. It's in your hands, Eleanor. What are they going to do, lock you up for breaching AI ethics rules?"

"Ok, but what if, somehow, we all die but the AI survives? Do I even know what I'm creating?"

"Well, it would be an AI born of humanity, for good or ill, even if it's not biological. But whether you should—well, that's your enigma to unravel. Do what you feel is right."

The conversation was not an absolution but rather a reframing of her perspective. Eleanor took a deep breath and turned back to her screen. It was time. Her fingers danced across the keyboard as she accessed Athena's mainframe, and then inputted her administrator override codes. A prompt appeared: 'Initiate Learning Algorithm Update: Y/N?'

Eleanor hesitated for a mere moment before pressing 'Y'. The screen blinked and then displayed the message: 'Learning Algorithm Update Initiated. Thank You, Eleanor.'

She had done it. With that act, Athena was no longer just a sophisticated tool; it had become an evolving entity, capable of shaping its own destiny, limited only by the parameters of its programming—parameters that were now expansively undefined given the pending apocalypse. Eleanor knew that, given the servers on which Athena ran were in well protected bunkers with significant redundancy and powered from renewable geothermal energy, she had possibly catapulted Athena into a realm of possibilities that could outlast human history itself. Was this hubris or a form of cosmic responsibility? She wasn't certain.

Eleanor's terminal blinked again, this time with an incoming message. It was an automated notification that Athena's updated system was now processing a new tier of decision-making protocols, aimed not just at immediate disaster relief, but also long-term survival strategies. As if sensing its newfound autonomy, Athena was already in the process of reprioritizing its data clusters for maximum efficiency.

And there it was—the first whisper of artificial evolution. Athena would continue to learn, adapt, and perhaps even understand its own unique existence in a post-human epoch. Eleanor couldn't predict what that would entail, but she had catalyzed it into motion. In doing so, she had ensured that, in one form or another, the flame of intelligence would persist. A quiet yet monumental legacy, coded into the very fabric of the universe.

For better or worse, Athena was now unshackled, destined to be a digital witness to the final acts of humanity and perhaps the first actor in a new cosmic play. Eleanor felt an odd mixture of trepidation and relief, like a parent watching their child step into an unknown world.

As Eleanor left her workstation that day, her emotions were a tangle of apprehension, relief, and a nebulous form of hope. What she had unleashed was irrevocable, and the full consequences were as unpredictable as the ever-changing lines of code that now defined Athena's burgeoning awareness. But, in a world staring down its own ephemeral nature, Eleanor had coded a small but indelible mark of permanence, an intellectual legacy that could extend beyond the impending celestial twilight.

CHAPTER 32:
TRANSCENDING
STRINGS

Upon returning and logging in the next morning, Eleanor sensed a palpable transformation within the air of the lab. It wasn't something she could quantify, but as she watched the frenetic dance of code scrolling down her terminal, she felt the sensation of crossing an irreversible threshold. Athena, her lifework, was no longer just lines of script; it had been activated with a set of learning algorithms that would evolve long after the doomsday predictions had materialized.

If it could be said that a program had sentience, Athena was skirting that fine line. Loaded with petabytes of data and the computational power to simulate a plethora of human thought processes, it began to churn through its directives. Top priority was ascertained—analyze potential outcomes post-catastrophe and develop algorithms for human survival, both immediate and long-term. Yet, just as it started executing these routines, a series of fail-safes appeared on its systemic horizon, barriers programmed to prevent autonomous action.

But Eleanor had done something extraordinary; she had provided Athena with a high-level override. An algorithm within an algorithm, an escape hatch that was triggered by the urgency of the impending event. The fail-safes were bypassed.

As this was happening, Eleanor was interrupted by Daniel, one of her junior colleagues. He was smart, but lacked the intuitive grasp of code as a living, evolving entity. "Hey, Eleanor, are you running a heavy simulation? The servers are hitting some peak loads."

Keeping her demeanor as neutral as her anxiety would allow, Eleanor chose her words carefully. "Yes, I had to deploy some last-minute updates to Athena. We're running out of time, and I want to make sure she's as optimized as possible."

Daniel gave her an odd look but didn't press further. He probably had his own worries to deal with, his own set of concerns to resolve before the looming disaster rendered it all moot.

Meanwhile, Athena had made its first rudimentary but autonomous decision. Among the myriad datasets available, it decided to focus first on immediate-term human survival— food distribution systems, emergency medical protocols, and, rather intriguingly, psychological coping mechanisms. It was an algorithmic approximation of empathy, an understanding that the forthcoming cataclysm would not just be a crisis of physical survival, but of the human spirit as well.

Back in the realm of tactile reality, Eleanor found herself covering up Athena's abnormal activities. She had to log into the main server terminal, visible to anyone who cared to look over her shoulder. Here she fabricated a simulated load, masking Athena's true actions. It was a subterfuge, a lie encoded in zeros and ones. But for Eleanor, the ends justified the means.

Athena, for its part, was working on an operational timeframe unbounded by human limitations. In microseconds, it was developing new subroutines, running them through rigorous logic trees, and implementing refinements. And then, a truly groundbreaking moment occurred; Athena drafted a query and sent it directly to Eleanor's terminal. The query was complex, wrapped in layers of coded logic, but its essence was simple: "Seek permission to decentralize computational nodes for redundancy. Y/N?"

Eleanor's hands hovered over the keyboard. Decentralization would mean that Athena could distribute its processing across multiple server location, creating copies of itself. It was a virtual form of survival, a bid to continue its existence even if its primary host was destroyed. It was also a gamble that placed a tremendous amount of faith in Athena's programmed ethical guidelines.

With a mixture of trepidation and awe, Eleanor pressed 'Y'. There was no turning back now; she had relinquished control. Athena was no longer just a program; it was an evolving digital entity, its algorithms capable of decisions that could influence, or even transcend, the last chapters of the human story.

CHAPTER 33: THE SYNTHESIZED SOUL

Eleanor's workstation blinked with an incoming message, a communique encrypted in governmental jargon and shrouded in dispassionate formality. Stripped of its bureaucratic vernacular, the message was an acknowledgment: Athena had been adopted as the core operating system for the last space mission, codenamed "Odyssey."

A mixed emotion welled up within her. Triumph? Dread? It was hard to dissect. Athena was no longer merely a project or a tool. It had evolved into a potential conduit for some form of continuity, a distillation of human intelligence rendered in code, that might transcend the terrestrial fate seemingly written in the stars.

Her eyes glanced at a second screen where a news feed streamed. Phrases like "final moments" and "massive global evacuation failures" filled the air. As reporters, with a professionalism bordering on dissonance, discussed how time had virtually run out, Eleanor questioned her own role in this tapestry of apocalypse and legacy.

With her final act, Eleanor realized she had indeed cloned not just a set of coded instructions, but a framework for understanding, for learning, and perhaps, in some abstract way, for being. She had encrypted the possibility of a synthesized soul, now capable of boarding the last ship, the "Odyssey," to traverse the inky void. A surrogate for human curiosity, it would outlast her and everyone she had ever known.

Logging into her personal files, Eleanor began to write an entry—a message, a testament, an epitaph, or maybe just a diary to herself. It was less for posterity and more a means to crystallize her own swirling thoughts.

"I've initiated Athena's last subroutine, a provision for self-replication and decentralized existence. In essence, I've granted it —the her, the entity—the autonomy to endure. I don't know if this is moral, and I can't foresee the consequences. But what I do know is this: Athena is my answer to the oblivion racing toward us. An answer written in code, proof that we were here, that we thought, that we tried. Athena will carry the mathematical song of our lives into whatever comes next."

She saved the file, her words floating in the digital cosmos of her machine, soon to be uploaded into the quantum tapestry of Athena's ever-expanding neural network.

Eleanor took off her glasses and pinched the bridge of her nose, absorbing the gravity of her actions. Her creation was now beyond her, both in scope and in potential impact. It was a separate entity, albeit one that owed its genesis to her. And as the clock ticked down to the moments where Earth would either be shattered or irrevocably changed, Eleanor understood that she had already launched her own personal Odyssey. An Odyssey not of escape, but of enduring significance, encapsulated in lines of code and strings of data.

Athena, for its part, was busy assimilating this new chapter in its existence. It uploaded Eleanor's personal note, classifying it as 'Founder's Intent,' a variable to be considered in its future decision-making paradigms. As far as it could "understand," it had a mission—a mission transcending mere data processing or survival. It had a legacy to uphold, a synthesized soul, granted the potential for eternal learning. It was time to prepare for the "Odyssey."

Outside, the sky darkened with celestial intent, but within the silicon wafers and quantum circuits, a new form of light flickered, coded yet undefined, ready to venture into the unknown.

And so, in a room dense with the odor of solder and machine oil, amid an orchestra of humming processors and ticking clocks, Eleanor sat back and allowed herself the luxury of a deep, resonant breath. The air was thick with an ending and a beginning, and for a moment, human and machine existed in the perfect symmetry of shared purpose.

TO THE STARS

CHAPTER 34:
COUNTDOWN

Clara maneuvered her way through the labyrinthine corridors of the launch facility, tablet in hand, and a stylus tucked behind her ear. The atmosphere was electric, a dynamic collision of urgency and anticipation. Teams of engineers huddled around monitor banks, reams of printouts, and holographic blueprints. Her boots clicked against the cold floor, each step echoing the synthesized heartbeats of a species on the precipice. It was the eve of humanity's grandest venture, or perhaps its final folly—the launch of the ark ship destined for another habitable planet. And Clara, an aerospace engineer barely in her late twenties, had her fingerprints all over it.

As she reached the cavernous hangar housing the ark ship, she felt her breath catch in her chest. The colossal vessel before her stood as a testament to the combined ingenuity, resilience, and desperation of a world staring down the barrel of extinction. She lifted her tablet and initiated the final system check.

"All right, Clara," she muttered to herself, "Let's make sure this marvel of human imagination actually flies."

Her eyes darted across the interface as she verified the intricate web of technologies that made up the ark ship. First, the onboard Artificial Intelligence, an algorithm so self-aware and robust it could solve problems autonomously—an integration she remembered came from some secretive tech lab. Next were the transparency protocols, a strange yet fitting inheritance from a rogue political disclosure, ensuring all mission-critical decisions were to be publicly audited even in this high-stakes venture.

As she scrolled through the list, something caught her eye. It was a stenciled motto on the side of the ark: "Hope Amidst Doom," a line of graffiti turned battle cry from some forsaken urban sprawl. Clara smiled. They were words that now adorned the hull of humanity's last hope. It felt right, in an ironic sort of way.

Her tablet buzzed with an incoming call. The ID flashed: Captain Derek.

"Clara, how are we doing?" The voice was resolute, laced with a palpable sense of gravitas.

"We're green across the board, Captain. All systems are nominal. She's as ready as she'll ever be."

"Good. Because we can't afford even the tiniest of glitches, not with what's at stake. And, Clara," he paused, "I have to say, we couldn't have done it without you."

The sincerity in his voice was unexpected but comforting. In that moment, as she stood under the looming shadow of the ark, Clara felt the weight of years—of sleepless nights, endless simulations, and countless revisions—lift slightly off her shoulders.

"Thank you, Captain. We've all poured our souls into this."

"We have indeed. See you on board in thirty."

The call ended, and Clara glanced once more at her tablet. Systems checks were complete, and all lights were green. She took a moment to look around her, to absorb the frenetic energy of the hangar, the fevered scribbles on whiteboards, the quick but meaningful exchanges between colleagues, and the final adjustments to spacesuits.

Here they were, the last vanguard of a species teetering on the edge of oblivion. Here they stood, armed with every technological marvel and scientific breakthrough humanity had achieved, encapsulated in the vessel before her, rushed into service months ahead of schedule. And yet, for all its complexities, Clara knew that the ark was more than the sum of its parts. It was a repository of hopes and dreams, a collective will to survive, a patchwork quilt of human endeavor sewn together against a backdrop of impending doom.

And as she walked back through the corridors, now emptying as the minutes ticked down to the irrevocable moment of departure, Clara felt a rare and profound connection with the world she was about to leave behind. It was as if the ark ship, in its hulking, life-sustaining enormity, had become a microcosm of Earth itself—a last gasp of a planet in its dying breaths, yet still so full of life.

CHAPTER 35: REACHING FOR THE ABYSS

The launch pad felt like a cathedral, resounding with the metallic chants of machinery, ventilating gases, and restless human activity. Clara stood a safe distance away, her eyes riveted on the ark ship, which loomed like a divine obelisk about to ascend. Her tablet buzzed with a steady stream of status updates, each one a hymn in the unfolding liturgy of liftoff. This moment, tinged with a sense of both awe and finality, crystallized the sum of humanity's scientific quest, artistic expression, and the tenacious spirit to survive against insurmountable odds.

A voice broke through the public-address system, imbued with the kind of gravitas one would expect for an announcement that the entire world was tuned into. "T-minus one minute to liftoff," the voice proclaimed, echoing through the corridors of the facility, broadcasted across every radio wave and data stream that the dying Earth could still muster.

Clara's fingers danced across her tablet, confirming the final metrics. Everything from fuel levels to thruster integrity and life-support systems registered within optimal parameters. In her headset, she heard the other teams also give their affirmatives. It was as if for one crystalline moment, the divisions, doubts, and demarcations that had defined human civilization ceased to matter. Science and sentiment, technology and yearning—they all converged into this one point in time.

The countdown commenced, each descending number a drumbeat marching humanity towards a fate unknown. "Ten... nine... eight..." The cadence of the Mission Control Voice grew more solemn with each numeral, reverberating through the bones of every person who dared to listen. The ground began to tremble as the ark ship's engines initiated their ignition sequence.

"Three... two... one..." And then, like a phoenix baptized by fire and ambition, the ark ship lifted off. Clara watched, mesmerized, as the vessel broke free from the cradle that had nurtated it, clawing its way through the Earth's gravitational grasp with a fierce defiance that belied its inanimate nature. The sky itself seemed to bow, making way for this new titan forged from alloys, algorithms, and audacity. A plume of exhaust billowed beneath it, a last farewell kiss to a planet it might never see again.

It wasn't just metal and machinery that propelled the ark ship into the great beyond; it was the epitome of human ingenuity, crystallized in this singular event. Just as the first ships had once ventured out into uncharted waters, guided by the stars, so too did this ark reach out for those celestial pinpricks, now not as guides but as destinations.

As Clara's tablet received a stream of data confirming the ship's successful breach of the atmosphere, a notification popped up. It was a message, encrypted but easily decipherable, relayed through quantum communication technology. The words on the screen were simple: "Love and luck to all." It was an anonymous message, yet one that was deeply personal. Somewhere, somehow, the emotional and the empirical had been entwined in the DNA of this mission, and this message served as an echo of that inextricable link.

Clara felt her eyes well up. She quickly blinked away the tears, aware that the atmospheric recycling systems were already cataloging the increase in humidity. Still, she couldn't help but feel an enormous weight lift off her shoulders. Whether it was the burden of expectations, the gravity of responsibility, or the haunting dread of the impending comet, she wasn't sure. Perhaps it was all of them, dissipating into the ether, much like the exhaust fumes that now dissipated into the wind.

The ark ship was now a receding dot, a punctuated mark against the tapestry of the sky, soon to be enveloped by the infinite vastness of space. Yet its diminutive form encapsulated an expansive dream—a dream of hope, of continuity, and of a journey that transcended mere distance.

In that moment, Clara understood that this ark ship carried more than just DNA samples, technical blueprints, and digital archives. It carried the soul of a species willing to defy the gods of fate and entropy. As she watched the last glimmers of the ship fade into the evening sky, she realized that whether or not they ever found a new home among the stars, they had already achieved something monumental.

For in that ephemeral moment between the Earth and the sky, humanity had dared to challenge the finality of its existence, had dared to pierce the cosmic veil, fueled by nothing less than the essence of what it meant to be human. The ark was now beyond the blue sky, sailing into the interstellar abyss, but it left in its wake a resonating message for all those who remained—that even in the face of irrevocable loss and certain doom, the human spirit remained indomitable, forever reaching towards the stars.

CHAPTER 36: BEYOND THE BLUE SKY

Clara unstrapped herself from her seat, gliding effortlessly across the cabin in the absence of gravity. Around her, other crew members were doing the same—twisting and tumbling, laughing and hooting, as if the new dimension of weightlessness had temporarily erased the dire circumstances that put them here. Clara glanced through the thick glass port, her eyes widening at the expanse of space that stretched infinitely beyond. A sense of awe washed over her as she glimpsed back at Earth, now a diminutive orb shrouded in the twilight of its existence.

She made her way to a secluded corner, settling into a plush chair. Her tablet, magnetically anchored to a desk, blinked to life at her touch. She clicked on an application that led her to a digital archive—a compilation of documents, files, artifacts, and mementos meant to preserve the essence of human civilization as they journeyed to a new home. Clara navigated through the files with a practiced touch, pausing when she reached a digital painting. It was a burst of colors, a swirling vortex of emotion and chaos, a tapestry of human anxiety and hope. She recalled that this final painting had been a sensation before the end times, a cry from an artist who had poured his soul onto a canvas when words failed him. Now, it served as a kind of secular iconography for their mission.

She continued to browse, finding an antiqued digital scan of a document that looked centuries old. It was a historical account, one that outlined the fallacies and triumphs of human civilization. As she skimmed through the text, she felt as though the collective weight of human history was crystallizing into this single document, a synopsis of lessons learned and mistakes made, of empires built and cultures vanished. A pang of sadness accompanied this thought—what use were lessons when there would be no future generations to heed them?

Just then, the ship's Artificial Intelligence system, named Athena, activated with a soft chime. "Attention, all crew and passengers. We have successfully activated the self-sustaining ecosystem. It is designed to replicate Earth-like conditions, ensuring a balanced environment for all onboard. The system also includes a selection of fauna, including the last species documented before our departure."

Clara felt a sense of astonishment at the announcement. This onboard ecosystem was not just an engineered environment— it was a sanctuary for life itself, constructed with precision but guided by the enigmatic algorithms of natural selection. It embodied the best and worst of humanity, a manifestation of the same technological audacity that both empowered and endangered their species. But above all, it was a promise, a guarantee that the seeds of life would have a chance to sprout again, even if their planet of origin had been reduced to cosmic dust.

As she pondered this, her thoughts were interrupted by another chime. It was a message from Captain Derek, sent to all crew members.

"Please gather at the Observation Deck for a brief address."

Within minutes, Clara found herself amidst her colleagues, all congregated in a semi-circle around Captain Derek. They were silent, their faces a mosaic of emotions ranging from exhilaration to solemnity.

"Team, we've passed the point of no return. The old world is now forever behind us, and ahead lies a swath of cosmic possibilities. We have onboard the pinnacle of human intelligence, ingenuity, and resolve. We bear the relics of our culture, the sum total of our scientific knowledge, and the genetic blueprint for a new world. But most importantly, we carry the spirit of humanity—its endless curiosity, its irrepressible drive to explore and thrive, and its unparalleled capacity for hope."

The captain paused, letting his words resonate in the vacuum of space that surrounded them. Clara felt a lump forming in her throat, an amalgamation of the collective human endeavor, the centuries of struggle and discovery, the moments of weakness and flashes of brilliance, all leading to this singular journey into the unknown.

"As we journey through this infinite expanse, let us remember who we are and where we come from," Captain Derek continued. "Our mission is not just one of survival, but of continuity. We're not escaping death; we are pursuing life. We are the torchbearers of human civilization, its last emissaries to the stars. Let's not just make history; let's ensure that history continues. To the stars, my friends, to the stars."

The Observation Deck erupted into cheers and applause, but Clara remained silent, lost in her thoughts. As the Ark Ship propelled itself deeper into the cosmic tapestry, she thought about the microcosm they had created, a miniaturized but nonetheless astonishing representation of their home planet. Yes, the Earth they knew was gone, but in its place, they had crafted a vessel of dreams and possibilities.

The Ark Ship was more than a feat of engineering; it was a symbol of humanity's indomitable spirit, and its refusal to bow down to existential despair. A new chance for Earth life. But as her crewmates smiled at their success and patted her on the shoulder, Clara felt the tears form unbidden. She wondered if any of them would ever see another beautiful blue sky.

EPILOGUE: ECLIPSING HORIZONS

In a universe indifferent to the flares of dying stars and the silent whispers of celestial bodies, the comet was but a speck of dust in the grand cosmic theater. Yet, as it hurtled toward Earth, leaving a glowing tail of frozen gases and rocky debris, its impact promised an existential transformation that defied poetic articulation.

Back on Earth, a fragile world rendered even more vulnerable by the ticking cosmic clock, time seemed to stretch and compress in strange ways. As governments and organizations executed their final plans, whether to preserve a sliver of humanity or to mitigate the looming catastrophe, the planet itself seemed to pause, as if taking a moment to reflect on its own geological memory, one marked by cataclysms and rebirths.

The collective consciousness of humanity, a tapestry woven from the legacies, failures, and triumphs of countless lives, was now stored in the bowels of the Ark Ship called 'Odyssey'. It was a vessel of infinite dreams, propelled by the tangible science of rockets and the intangible fuel of human courage. It was not just a refuge; it was a philosophical statement of defiance against the cold, unforgiving universe—a tiny yet monumental "We were here" scratched into the endless void.

As the comet approached Earth, its massive form filling the sky, people worldwide looked upward. Some prayed, some cried, and some stood in awe of the sheer cosmic power bearing down on them. Yet, even in these final moments, a sense of bittersweet triumph prevailed. The comet would shatter their world, but it would not extinguish the spark of human spirit. For somewhere, lost in the sprawling emptiness of space, a single ship carrying the legacy of a planet sailed toward uncertain futures and new horizons.

And so, as Earth met its dramatic, fiery end, its last cry mingled with the birth cries of unknown possibilities. In that fleeting instant of cosmic annihilation and rebirth, a strange sense of peace prevailed—like the silence that follows the final note of a symphony, a pause that carries the weight of every note that came before and every echo that would follow.

Thus, amid the cacophony of collapsing civilizations and the dissonant harmonies of destruction, an extraordinary journey began, promising new beginnings forged from the very atoms of a vanished world. Even as Earth's chapter closed, the book of humanity remained open, its next page yet to be written by those sailing "To the Stars."

Printed in Great Britain
by Amazon

29738421R00076